My Best Friend

Hildegard

My Best Friend

Hildegard

Adam Greenberg

dangerous angel

dangerous angel

For

Abby
Adrian
Amanda
Francesca
Jill
Michael
Rhani

My Best Friend

Hildegard

Part I

Hildegard

he shopped at the department stores of Hell, bought tons of fine clothing studded with jewels and flower petals, crowns and earrings pierced with shards of platinum and diamonds. She allowed her demon lovers, painfully gorgeous elf-like charming drunken rich college student slackers, to wine and dine her and take her on thrilling dates, driving her through midnight countrysides in their evil-looking convertibles on warm summer ghostly nights. Phillip, a rich college slacker from Iowa, wore a golden hoop earring like a pirate, and looked ageless with twinkling, disarming eyes, staring as if penetrating. His expensively slummy clothing sagged around an attractive clavicle and upper chest, tiny hairs like slivers of gold flecking out the v-neck shirt. He

promised her the world, his world, his hell, his riches. Phillip had a certain immaturity that was both captivating and embarrassing. He fancied himself an intrepid adventurer, and Hildegard found his self-absorption rather annoying.

Still, he gave his demon heart passionately to her, and she fucked him over and over again in the bungalows of a dingy lamplit tavern in the marshes of a mosquito-infested paradise where they roamed daily, drunk, shaken, naked, shameless. Hildegard's laugh and smile, wickedly tapered breasts and sense of humor made Phillip feel elated. He gazed at her constantly with loving preciousness in his face. Hildegard pleasured him to his heart's desire and felt genuine love for Phillip, although she knew that soon she would break his heart.

One day Hildegard walked in on Phillip and me fucking. Our bodies under those dusty gray sunbeams streaming in the arched windows of my monastery cell. Phillip was fuck fuck fucking me with abandon, abandoning all sense of propriety, all sense of respect for my being, even. That was simply how we fucked, Phillip and I. As if our bodies were nothing but knives and rags mingling inhumanly in the immaculate sheets of my cell. "Johnny, you exquisite thing, how I covet you," he would whisper.

Phillip's existence had only become apparent to me in stages; I have no idea how we came to be aware of each other. He disguised himself as an ordinary young monk when he came to visit, always doing work in the kitchen, scrubbing pots and pans and broiling up disastrously delicious stews, muttering the most ecstatic prayers as he stirred and stirred and stirred over the flame. About twice a week he would barge into my cell with a piping hot pot of stew, wake me up abruptly and spoon feed me the runny globs that burnt the inside of my mouth, before fucking me. Phillip was my first lover. Our relationship was based on sex and trickery that bordered on abuse. I believe to this day that Phillip was an actual demon, devoid of humanness, and he owed his corporeal existence on the earth to Hildegard's one-pointed concentration. After her initial encounter with him in a dream, I could hear her repeatedly chanting his name during her prayers, like any other obsessed teenage girl, except the demonic fire in her eyes was real and unwavering. Sometimes I wonder if Hildegard herself wasn't partly spawned from somewhere else. In any case, after my sleepless nights convulsing with Phillip, I'd often wake up with a throbbing head and parched tongue, grasping for his vanished body, wondering if it had all been a wonderful nightmare. . . until I spied the spilled gruel puddles on the floor, like congealed vomit, and savored the secret that I'd had a true encounter with my demon lover.

When Hildegard first found out that I'd been fucking around with Phillip, she had a fit, spitting and cursing in the courtyard. Everyone assumed this was one of her usual fits of ecstasy, although normally her face was more serene and zombielike, and her vocalizations slightly less violent. Afterwards, people close by would usually feel a momentary sense of peace, and often sick kids in the infirmary would find their illness had disappeared. This time was way different—her face was red with a deep crevice between the eyes, and her movements were jerky and spastic. She was shouting broken Latin phrases that were mostly incomprehensible, but I swear I could make out the words "banish" and "slay." With her reputation for ecstatic fits, Hildegard could get away with almost any weird behavior. Anyway, no one seemed to look twice.

For days afterward, Hildegard ignored me. When I tried to approach her or get her attention from across the dining hall, her eyes appeared made of stone. What abuse I suffered during those days of torment! Hildegard could be so selfish—she had plenty of ethereal as well as fleshly lovers, why should she begrudge me an affair with just one of them? It made me sick, since she knew how I had longed and longed for love, someone to rip my body apart every night in my sleep, someone to whisper prayers of love and devotion in my ear, etc.

I had confessed all this to her three years ago, when we were thirteen. It was during our first late night philosophical dorm conversation. We'd talked into the dead of night about love, existence, robotic society, marvelous archangels who wear slippers more radiant than the lightning which destroys time and space, and all sorts of other childish things. I told her of my perpetual state of heartbreak, how my emotional life had never been anything but ravenous longing and certainty that no amount of love or affection, even from God or the angels, would ever be enough.

Hildegard looked at me amazingly, like a sorceress penetrating my bones. Her eyes glazed over, then sharply refocused on me. "Your pain, your longing is a gift," she said. "It is divine pain, longing, discontent, and it is burning all your hindrances. Your heart is so unencumbered by the shackles of Satan, that no amount of affection can ever satisfy you anyway. Your fierce Love of the Void makes you insatiable."

I usually hate when people do that, take an obvious deficiency and try to glamorize it as if it's the best thing in the world. But she was kind of convincing. It made me feel both weirdly peaceful and wrenched apart by grief. I then expressed to her my deepest wish for a boyfriend.

Hildegard closed her eyes and took a long pause. I found it a little presumptuous that she was acting this way, as if I were consulting an oracle. Which I wasn't. I was simply trying to bond with my new friend. It seemed ridiculous that she needed to close her eyes and take these long, melodramatic pauses just to have a late night dorm conversation. But I went along with it.

Hildegard went on: "You will attract all varieties of lovers, and they will adore you and bless you, for the love you can give is inexhaustible. And though you will suffer continuous pain and grief even as you love, your gift to them will be the revelation of the true nature of God, for only God's Presence and God's Love are limitless."

I really didn't know what to make of all this. I guess she was giving me a compliment, but it sounded pretty tragic. We just sat there looking at each other. I didn't feel pressured to say anything, which was a relief. Part of me thought Hildegard was totally pretentious, but at least she didn't seem to need any validation. Not like those obnoxious common soothsayers on the plaza who were always desperately trying to get someone to listen to them. We sat there on her bed listening to midnight raindrops on the tall pointed windowpanes.

Then Hildegard stood on her bed and reached upwards. Her dorm room had all manner of winged sculptures hanging from the ceiling. She plucked a winged mermaid from its string, and presented it to me. Swordlike amethyst crystals jutted out of the huge Egyptian eyes.

"I want you to have this," Hildegard said. "It's to draw love to you."

And now, three years later, she was pissed that I stole her beautiful demon. These lovers just swarmed around her, and she didn't even like him that much. I really couldn't believe Hildegard's selfishness sometimes.

Page Coin

he next day, I took the ferry across the river to Whole Foods. I was so burnt out and exhausted from the dramatic events of the previous day—Hildegard walking in on me and Phillip, not to mention my inescapable chronic insomnia, that I felt almost chipper. Without thinking, without tasting, I robotically snacked from a bag of candy-coated pretzels I had packed for the ferry ride. My main religious teacher, Brother Raoul, would not be happy with me. He was always counseling me to eat with total awareness and moderation. Every other bite I would toss a bit of pretzel into the water and watch as the black doves of the forest swooped down to gobble them up. Such a greedy world.

As I disembarked, the banks of the river

were alive with the colors and moods of spring. A mother of a bright face played with her little children, and flowers danced around merrily. The sun warmed me and the fog beckoned me toward the forest, the path that led deep within, to Whole Foods.

Our local Whole Foods was sort of a cross between a castle and a library. Cute guys were always shopping there, but I was usually too nervous to talk to them. It's hard to make the first move when you're feeling desperate. I just knew they'd be able to tell that I cared too much. The one time I'd had the courage, it was a blonde leprechaun of a guy, with an almost nauseatingly beautiful smile, dressed in mint green. He seemed really flattered but turned out to be straight. Just my luck. Since that disappointing encounter, I hadn't been able to muster the courage to approach anyone else.

I walked up the stone path to the castle, bristling with bird songs and the babbling of a brook. A fancy lady in sunglasses and suede, with a long brown pony tail, walked past me, carrying a bag of groceries. Other than that, no one was around. I peered into her bag, a habit of mine. Wild arugula, canned salmon and some cakey dessert.

I swung open the heavy oak doors, arching high above. It was a gorgeous day at Whole Foods. Everyone seemed happy, content somehow. The guys in produce were singing to themselves as they set out the first nectarines of the season. There was mist in the aisles. I saw some goth middle school kids stick their hands in the bulk candy and look around to see if anyone saw.

I really didn't have anything to do there, I wasn't hungry anymore after all those pretzels I'd had on the ferry. So I just kind of wandered through the corridors of the castle peeking around, sort of half-bored and half-sick from eating too many pretzels. I really didn't feel like myself. I felt like a dolphin out of my element, walking among strange beasts that called themselves human beings.

There have been times when a black-winged demon of melancholy forced itelf close to me. There were times when I was so sick, from having eaten so many pretzels, that I couldn't leave the house. I'd dream of visiting Whole Foods on those days, of feeling free finally. Finally. Finally. Now here I was, roaming the aisles with nothing to do.

I startled to find myself staring at the profile of a curiously charming young man completely engrossed in the cookie section. He was turning around in his hand a small tin box of chocolate covered biscuits shaped like angels of the apocalypse. His lips protruded gently like rose petals and his brown hair swept casually halfway down his face. I must have stood there mouth agape for at least a minute, but he was so engrossed in his cookies that he didn't notice.

"These are really good," I said with a contrived casual enthusiasm as I pointed to another box of cookies near him, butter biscuits sandwiched between fudge diamonds.

The guy looked up sweetly and smiled, open to my remark. He picked up the box I'd indicated and examined it. "Hmmm, looks really good," he said. "Now I can't decide!" He looked at me again, perplexed. His outlandish outfit and transparently thin ears made me suspect he was of eldritch blood.

For some reason, a bolt of courage shook through me. "Why don't you get that one, I'll get this one, and we can go have a picnic together?"

"Like, right now?" he asked uncomfortably. He seemed doubtful. Clearly probably not interested, but at this point I was too exhausted to care.

"Yes, right away!" I declared. "I'm in the mood for cookies. I love cookies. I can't get enough cookies. I cry cookies when I'm depressed and I shit cookies when I'm glad. Let's make merry with cookies for the time being, my whole life is in a shambles!"

To be honest, I didn't say all those things, although that was my sentiment. Whatever I said, though, he got my point and shrugged, as if to say, "Why not?" and without any further conversation, we went through the checkstand together, and out the door.

As we walked behind the castle, toward the bank of the babbling brook, he asked me my name.

"Johann Hofmannfrei," I replied. "You?"

"Page Coin," he answered. What a hot name. And an exciting sparkle in his eyes.

A moment later, we were comfortably situated in the dappled shade of a blooming jacaranda. Page Coin had graciously removed his cape and laid it on the grass, like a royal green velvet picnic blanket. I was nervous, but managed to keep my cool, as far as I can tell. We didn't really talk much, just ripped our way through both boxes of cookies. As delicious as they were, by the third cookie they tasted like nothingness in my mouth. I still managed to help him put an end to them.

Page Coin smiled and his teeth were full of chocolate. This disgusted me and I felt sick from eating too much. What should I do? I told myself not to sabotage this encounter. After a few more minutes of polite, strained conversation, I told him I had to go.

"But wait," Page protested. "When can I see you again?"

I scribbled my true name on a piece of paper. With knowledge of this name, he would be able to contact me in my dream.

Back at school, I was out in the courtyard at lunch, with the skinny shark boys who were squinting and ravaging their lunch with their teeth. O how I wish they would ravage me too, I'd give anything to be torn apart like the lunch of a gorgeous lad! The sun was beating down on the dry grass. I missed Hildegard. We still hadn't made up. Was she still mad? Seriously, how dare she.

I went to the vending machine, but none of those evil candies were enticing me. So I joined Lucia and some of the acting kids I got along with, but never felt like I knew at all. They talked in contrived voices and laughed about nothing. Hildegard came up to us and started bragging about her new herb garden. She looked at everyone but me, so it was obvious she was still mad. She went on and on about how she'd had a vision that the sky turned into a hole and out of the hole came drops of blood, which landed on the rectangle of dead land next to the cemetery. Nothing ever happened on that barren, cracked land behind the abbey, except certain of our unappealing classmates were said to have made out there, like carrion crows in the dirt. How that happens, I have no idea, but if they actually managed to get some action, I can see no place more fitting than by that boneyard. According to Hildegard's vision, the large drops of blood fell upon that plot of land and made it fertile. So when she got up, she planted some bachelor's button and panic grass there and sure enough, the garden was thriving overnight.

"Who cares," I said. "Panic grass is a truly unremarkable weed."

Without even a glance towards me, Hildegard finished with some niceties to the others, and then turned and walked away. I just couldn't deal with this fight, so I followed her to her cloister. Usually Hildegard spent the last 20 minutes of lunch in prayer. She completely ignored me as I walked behind her, then brusquely grabbed the doorknob and turned back at me like a petty vipress. "What? Don't look at me in such a way."

"What way? I wasn't even looking at you in 'a way.' Anyway, I don't care about your stupid visions."

Hildegard scowled, then rolled her eyes and swung the door open, inviting me in. She told me she was totally over the fact that I had slept with her demon. We both laughed as we realized how stupid Phillip was. Totally neither one of our styles. I still desperately wanted to fall in love one day, for real. A deep, lasting love with someone I could actually respect. As for Hildegard, she was in love with God, and her relationships with others, even the saints and archangels, were merely trinkets.

The Earl of Brothershead

hat week, the Earl of Brothershead was stopping at our school as part of a lecture tour he was doing all around Europe. It was just a drawn-out advertisement for his lame bilberry extract and network marketing scheme. I don't understand why our school makes us go to these despicable assemblies. The earl was really fake and annoying, with excessively ruffled clothing and hair styled in a wavy tonsure with lots of gel.

His talk was all about the healing power of bilberry extract, and he bragged non-stop about his "unprecedented, proprietary cold-extraction method." Didn't he know that the ancient Egyptians had figured out how to cold-extract bilberry over 5000 years ago? Anyway, Hildegard was avidly taking notes and kept shushing me when I tried to interject a witty remark or distract her in some way from the fascinating Earl of Brothershead. Usually when we had a lame assembly like this, Hildie and I would be in the back making an utter mockery of it, or finding other ways to entertain each other through the morbidity of sitting there. But she could be unpredictable, and on this particular day, she somehow wanted to geek out to this clown's lofty words about the magnificent bilberry. Seriously, I don't want to dwell on it, but that shit was so hilarious that I gotta recapture some of it here. He went on and on:

"Bilberry Bliss is not a company, it's a member-centric rewards lifestyle. It's fun, and good for you. And the more involved you get, the more rewards you rack up. When you sign up and join the family, we'll give you a rose with a tassel, plus lots of samples. At the second level, you get a gift basket full of surprises! And when you get to the third level, you will definitely go to heaven when you die. The fourth through eleventh levels will determine how close you will sit to God in the assembly hall, and there are lots of other incentives! Elite gold members get to go on a private cruise with Saint Ambrose every year. Bilberry extract is absolutely THE most versatile, delicious, and beneficial medicine in the world. A new study by the Vatican indicates that it effectively treats depression, apathy, fear of death, pride, homosexuality, and a whole host of other spiritual diseases."

Saint Ambrose? Personally, I would rather go to hell than go on a cruise with him.

One girl sitting in the front row raised her hand to say that she was very inspired by the earl's talk about the health benefits of bilberry extract, but found that whenever she took it she felt sick.

"You have to understand that bilberries are an advanced synergy—much more than just a food. This is spiritual stuff," he said with a condescending grin. "So if you find it makes you sick, you probably just aren't ready for it yet." He winked nauseatingly.

At this point I glanced at Hildegard to see what she was making of this bullshit. She continued to scribble away at her paper, and it was then that I realized she wasn't listening to the lecture at all—she was fervently at work on something else. Something with illegible words and diagrams. I couldn't quite make it out over her shoulder, and I didn't want her to notice my attempts. I was left somewhat irked and abandoned to suffer this lecture alone, while she scrawled out notes on her otherworldly visions, or took musical dictations from angels, or invented sexual fantasies to be carried out later with as-yet-nonexistent entities, or whatever she was doing.

Danny Barnaby

s usual, I couldn't sleep. Lying awake in bed completely desperate for rest, of course around 3am I became ravenous. I snuck down to the chapel to try to find some communion wafers or something, anything to put in my mouth. I needed to consume some inert substance that could hopefully somehow decrease my sense of being awake and alive.

The entire body of the church, like the body of a wild animal, was full of naked beings with dazzling flesh performing all kinds of unions together. Hildegard, emanating red light, was thrusting herself on a handsome hunky angel, bright burgundy in color, whose wide open mouth, nostrils and eyes seemed to express great torment or surprise, although I know, as I have been constantly reminded in dreams, my perception is flawed. I was strongly attracted to the guy, but I couldn't stand to watch them, so I immediately looked away. I made it to the supply cupboard amid the clanging and bellowing heavenly voices of all those beings shoving each other around, and I seized a long plastic sleeve full of communion wafers stacked one on top of the other. Recalling that I had a quarter of a jar of almond butter under my bed, I rushed out the back of the church to avoid the scene. Some of those beings definitely noticed me, completely uncaringly consumed by their bliss, but I'm pretty sure Hildegard didn't. Anyway, she never mentioned it afterwards. The crisp wafers were the perfect thing slathered in almond butter, but I cannot imagine how they would compare to Hildegard's blisses.

I myself had no such bliss at all. All I had was a hopeless crush on a boy named Eliano. He would let me flirt with him, but when it got too intense, he would distance himself. Then I would give up and ignore him, and he would act all interested again. It went on like that forever. We went biking around, down to the beach and up by the old falling apart cemetery, and then into the woods. I kept asking myself, is this a date? We saw a treehouse across the river. I normally don't feel like jumping into a cold river when it's already cold and the sun's going down, but I wanted to prove how fun-loving and impulsive I am, so I suggested we swim across to the treehouse. I was cold and wet and excited, shaking with fear and infatuation. But we made it across, both apparently so afraid to show our scrawny bodies that we left our shirts on and got all sopping wet and freezing. As we climbed up the ladder, I was still acting as if I did this kind of adventurous thing all the time, but it turned out the treehouse was full of spiders and splinters, and it was getting late. So we didn't go in.

My one-sided romance with Eliano was weird and sad, but things were even weirder and sadder around school. One girl, Sabrina Meier, tragically died after giving birth to a skeleton. She'd gotten pregnant, but was afraid of being violently punished when the teachers found out. So she tried to give herself an abortion by wearing a tight corset all the time, and taking these weird herbs she got from a blind herbalist she met at the bottom of a swamp. Thanks to the combination of the corset and herbs, Sabrina retained the fetus for three whole years. During that time, the fetus' flesh had decomposed but the bones continued to grow. Finally, Sabrina discharged the skeleton, but by then it was the size of a toddler and mortally wounded her on the way out. A totally preventable tragedy.

This kind of thing seemed to be happening more and more often at our school—good kids dying or going insane for no good reason, because of either the administration's direct cruelty, or just from the general oppressive atmosphere.

I mean, wtf? Everyone knows it's a terrible idea to get abortion drugs and advice from some random creepy lady at the bottom of a swamp, but that's just the kind of thing any normal, upstanding citizen might do under an oppressive regime. Often you would find body parts out in the trash bins in the alley, and kids had gone missing. There was a wicked possessing spirit everywhere. It really sucked, especially for a sensitive kid such as myself.

Hildegard ditched class all the time, and she never got in trouble because the fathers were scared of her. Besides, she was responsible for our school choir's fame and awards in competitions. In Junior year, she started going away for days at a time. No one ever asked where she went or what she was doing, but she'd come back with this bizarre, incredible music for the choir. It sounded like winding smoke and alien orgasms, and was so beautiful I almost couldn't stand to listen to it.

One night we were sitting on Hildie's bed. She was working on some commentary on one of her visions (did the teachers ever make her do any real homework?), and I was trying to force myself to start a terrible paper on the abomination of postnihilist magisteriae. Of course, I couldn't say what I actually believed, cause I'd get an F and probably get kicked out of school or murdered. So I was just sitting there procrastinating and resenting the whole thing.

Hildegard looked up and told me she was going to be away for a few days. And that I should watch the grounds around the cemetery. Should any spirits arise there, I should help them to their destinations.

"I wish I could go with you for once," I said with a sigh.

"You belong here, Johnny, and you're the only one I trust to be helpful. Everyone else around here is full of shit in one way or another, but you actually have a good heart. And you need to start helping out all the lost beings."

"Are you expecting anyone?" I asked.

"Beings are always arising and disappearing. Can I trust you to not get distracted?"

"Ok," I said.

I didn't even start my paper. I fell asleep on top of Hildegard's bed.

I woke up at 3:45 am. She was already gone. I looked out the window just in time to see the bloodred limo drive away.

I never asked too many questions about Hildegard's other life. It made me uncomfortable to know too much. I feel so limited in this flesh, yet she is able to explore beyond the confines of reason. I almost can't bear my limitations. Still, one perfect earthly body to love would be enough to help me bear all the world's sins and shortcomings. I went through the day bleary and tired.

Next morning I woke at 3:03 am. Why do I have to be alive at this hour? Since it was obvious I wouldn't get back to sleep, I took a walk out behind the abbey.

From the distance, from beyond the cemetery, the burning grounds where the heathens incinerate their dead, a being came. Hiding the shadow of a tree, I watched him pass. He was a kid about my age, with ashes sweeping through his hair. I felt like I was supposed to talk to him, but I didn't know what to say.

The guy was new at school and showed up in my first-period Social Studies class. He had a very severe face, like jutting knobs and knives, with brilliant eyes in dark sunken holes. No one knew him. His name was Danny Barnaby. I was mesmerized by his self-righteous ugliness, which appeared noble.

I couldn't focus in class, and I kept looking at Danny. I wanted to see if he was looking at me. When I saw that he was at one point, I jerked my head away. I can't believe I did that, it was so obvious! . . . I still couldn't help myself from looking over at him continuously. Anyway, it was better than watching Brother Miklaus jump around the class like an idiot, spouting nauseating propaganda—which he seemed to actually believe—about the crusaders bringing peace and passing out applesauce to the heathens, who were starving because they didn't believe in God. Danny and I finally met each other's glance and rolled our eyes at Brother Miklaus' inane antics. But when the bell rang, I was swept up in the chaotic movement of bodies, and didn't get a chance to talk to him.

At lunch, Danny was eating alone in the shady stone arcade outside the library. He was scowling and reading some battered philosophical book. His black T-shirt had a picture of two skeletons with crescent moons for heads making out, and excessively flowery calligraphy that said "Jester & Lunette"—undoubtedly some obscure, pretentious, literary darkwave band. Danny seemed really unapproachable, so everyone left him alone.

I just decided to go up to him, probably emboldened by lack of sleep. "Hey, I'm Johnny," I said in a tone that actually sounded confident and relaxed.

"Hey. Danny."

We bonded over how supremely atrocious our Social Studies class was.

"Are all the teachers here as pointless as that guy?"

"Pretty much," I said.

"But I mean, aren't there any adepts here? I'm looking for spiritual masters."

I can't imagine why he would expect to find "spiritual masters" at Disibodenberg. I mean, Saint Eucharius supposedly used to ride through here on his red horse on Christmas Eve and pass out wish-granting lockets to the children. But that was like 500 years ago. Anyway, the children all became wicked, using their powers to steal each others' bodies to commit nonvirtuous acts, etc, accumulating mountains of sin on which they built temples to corrupt gods and generally making a mess of life.

"Sorry man, no masters here. If you want to find spiritual masters, you'd probably have to go to Alexandria or somewhere like that."

Danny looked annoyed, even offended. "Alexandria? That's the perfect place to go if all you want is to see a bunch of overeducated idiots from around the world debating semantics and spouting scripture with no idea of what any of it actually means! But not everything in religion is bullshit, you know. I want to learn the real stuff."

"Like what? How to become one with God or something?" I asked.

Danny laughed. "I hate God," he said.

"I don't believe in God," I said.

Danny's face became even more contemptuous and dark. "God exists, Johnny, you can be sure of that. It's very unpleasant to think about, so I can undertand you not wanting to believe. But reality definitely exists, and it's a disgrace!" He emphasized his words by jerking his arms around. "And the essence of all that is God. GOD. He made all this!" He flung his arms around even more wildly to make sure I understood that all manifest existence was included.

Really. I considered this for a second. Maybe Danny was onto something, but he was acting all out of hand with it. His face truly looked like a cold chiseled piece of metal hardware, as if parts of it would start to violently break off and go flying around if his expression got any harsher.

"Well, why don't you just kill yourself, then?" I suggested.

Danny laughed demonically. "I wish it were that easy!" he practically shouted. Our conversation was starting to attract attention from other kids eating their lunch, and he was totally oblivious. "If I thought death actually existed, I would kill myself in an instant! Unfortunately, it wouldn't change anything."

WTF. I didn't really have anything to say to that.

"Really, Johnny, haven't you read any spiritual literature? Death isn't even real. . . after this body dies, there's something else, then something else, it just goes on and on and on. . . but I'm definitely going to find a way out!" he concluded victoriously. Just then, in perfect cinematic timing, the bell rang.

It was amazing to me how when Danny was talking about how much he hated everything and how horrible everything was, he actually seemed the most alive. When Hildegard got back that night, I told her about him. The three of us started eating lunch together.

Weekend of Endless Days

"ou guys should definitely fuck," Hildegard said to us one day. "I don't understand what you're waiting for, it's obviously going to happen sooner or later."

What? Danny and I just sat there uncomfortably. Although somewhat intrigued by Danny's morose passion, I had a sexual aversion to his face and body and self. At best, it would be like having sex with a brick.

Still, I liked that Danny had been joining us for lunch lately. He insisted on spending so much of his free time in his room, meditating for hours. I don't think he ever got anywhere with it, because he was always irritable and upset. But he seemed determined to experience something more than this drab existence.

Once I asked Danny why he had to spend so

much time alone, and I complained about how lonely I got when Hildegard was away. At least her pursuits of other realms are successful, I thought, but kept it to myself.

Danny snapped at me. "I have no interest whatsoever in the petty prizes of this world, and that includes friends." Then he calmed down a little, and in a rare moment of self-awareness, seemed to realize how obnoxious he was being. "I'm sorry," he said, still with a harsh edge. "You're really cool, and you and Hildegard are the only people here I'd choose to hang out with. But I think I'm really meant to spend more time alone."

I didn't take Danny's words too personally, because he was usually disagreeable, and I had mixed feelings about him anyway. After that conversation, though, he did seem to spend more time with us.

One night, Danny and I were sitting in my room. Ever since Hildegard had said that thing about Danny and me fucking, I had tried to think of him in a sexual way. I didn't have any desire for him whatsoever, but I started wondering if I could possibly develop some. At least with Danny, I might have a chance—unlike Eliano, whose adorable existence simply mocked my desire.

Danny was gabbing enthusiastically about the red monks of Bernkastel—starving beggar-monks who lived in a little camp by the Rhine, until wicked Queen Baldechildis vowed to eliminate religion from the country. Some of her soldiers snatched up one of the monks and slit his throat in front of the others. When the other monks saw this, the Holy Spirit entered them, and in an ecstatic rage, they began to rip apart the soldiers with their bare hands. The monks voraciously drank all the soldiers' blood, as well as their slain companion's, until not a single drop was left. But rather than satiate their hunger, this activity only made them even more voracious. So ensued an orgy of the whole gathering ripping one other apart in a grand feast that went on for several days, or according to some accounts, several world ages (during which a universe is destroyed and created a number of times). After that incident, the monks found that they manifested stigmata, which ceaselessly flowed blood with miraculous healing properties. Known as the red monks of Bernkastel, they traveled all across Germany, feeding their stigmata-blood to lepers and other sick and destitute outcasts. Danny talked about them with such sincere admiration that I actually started to see some beauty in him, and I wondered if fucking and loving him might be easier than I'd thought.

We were sitting on my bed, our backs resting against the wall. A few long moments after Danny stopped talking, I put my foot on his shin. For another long moment, he didn't react at all. Then he looked at me. I'm so sick of pretending and trying to get guys to like me.

"Do you think Hildegard's right?" I asked him. I was still not brave enough to just start putting my arms all over him.

"About what?" he asked, as if he didn't know what I was talking about.

"Well, come on, you said yourself that this world is basically a heap of trash and corpses. We're walking zombies, pretending to be alive. Do you want to try sex?"

For the first time, I saw Danny smile in a completely relaxed way, with no trace of irony or contempt. I took this as an invitation to proceed. There was nothing to lose. It would be like an experiment.

I moved my fingers over Danny's blue T-shirt. The whole thing felt really contrived and I didn't know what I was doing. Making love with a demon is much easier cause you forget who you are and don't even know that you're doing it while it's happening. Plus, Phillip was actually incredibly sexy. Touching Danny felt totally unerotic.

I put my hands under his shirt and felt his ribs. He just kind of let me touch him at first, then put his arms around me and touched my back lightly.

His nipple was cold. That was about all I could take.

"I'm sorry," he finally said. "There's no life in this body for sex."

"Ok," I said, relieved.

Then he went off to do his meditation practice.

Hildegard and I were in my drab dorm room on an almost rainy day. She was busy scribbling away on something as usual and I was sitting there doing nothing, but feeling slightly cold and drowsy. Her pelvis was a sun and I was her friend, a dragon. When I woke up, there was a drop of blood between my eyes.

All of a sudden, Hilegard slammed her notebook closed and got up. "Ok, let's go," she said, startling me out of my daze.

"Where are we going?" I love how she always

assumes I'll do whatever she says without any explanation.

"We're going to the mall. I need ribbons."

On the way out of the dorm, we stopped by Danny's room and convinced him to take a break from his morose alone-time battling with existence. He acted like it was a huge inconvenience, but obviously he wanted to come with us.

The mall was a pointed building called the Tower, not unlike a large full breast, which dominated the downtown plaza. Ordinarily, to get there from our school, one would walk for about half an hour down a dusty highway, with scarcely a tree for decoration. I hated that walk. Hildegard had recently done a routine exorcism for a wealthy patron who lived on the river, and he had given her a key to his gate. So we were able to take a shortcut through a pleasant and opulent series of parks, with streams and gazebos and everything. We were there in half the time.

There was so much at the mall, so much to delight an idiot's senses. It was kind of fun to be out and around, with all the uncaring mothers, children parasites born of filth demanding rainbow sprinkle cookies, and so on. Pretty young plump goth shop girls giving Hildegard ugly eyes. Cardigans hanging on racks like drab victims, tired spaced-out food court workers in disgraceful uniforms. Everything of hate. Why do I always gotta be so negative about stuff? I don't want to be a monk, I want to be a lover. Compassion is all that matters in this fucked up world. Compassion and compassionate sex.

Suddenly I spotted Jenna Forrester coming out of Starbucks with her cronies, Skipper and Spencer. A trio of ugly snobs who fancied themselves desirable trendsetters. Jenna was wearing brown vinyl tights with a yellow faux fur pussy. Truly disgusting. Skipper and Spencer were wearing short shorts and striped shirts and hats in different colors, and both chattering away with the same vapid gay accent, as if that made them the world's most perfect gay couple. The three of them scurried eagerly into Abercrombie, like manic tarantulas.

Danny disappeared into the bookstore. And I didn't feel like following after Hildegard. I put my feet onto a vibrating massage thing at Brookstone.

Danny found me there ten minutes later. He was eager to show me what he'd just bought—some self-help/philosophy book based on Saint Eucharius's Antidote to the Counterfeit

Spirit's Generation of Bodies. "This is the real stuff, Johnny," Danny said as he handed it to me.

I opened it at random: ". . . To perfectly accomplish the 'Sublime Ruin' which is in fact a metaphorical vestment employed by that thing which ordinary beings call "the real," or, even worse, "the unreal," the true disciple of the Endless must paradoxically, and with courage, employ phallic vision even to the very End. . ."

That was enough for me to get an idea of Danny's reading material. I don't understand what he finds so fascinating and useful about reading all those words that don't have anything to do with each other. Or with life. Or with dreams.

We went to Orange Julius and I ordered a grape Julius. "I want to throw it all away," I told Danny, referring both to my Julius and also my life in general.

We trailed off in search of Hildegard, but she was nowhere to be seen. We had no trouble, however, spotting Jenny Forrester again, whose tragic bright yellow cooch couldn't be missed. Really, the sight of her with Skipper and Spencer, now with arms full of disgusting shopping bags, was enough to nearly make me barf all over the mall tile. I introspected as to why this might be so—am I jealous? Do I secretly fear that I'm as disgusting as that bunch? Do I just hate everyone? Why can't I just be happy and enjoy myself at the mall like everyone else? No matter how ugly they are, they all seem to have boyfriends. Why won't Eliano fall in love with me? Why can't I act natural around him? Am I putting too much pressure on myself to be a certain way? He's so beautiful it physically hurts to be around him! Are my standards too high? Why is everyone so depressing and stupid? Why am I so ugly and unsuited to this world?

We finally found Hildegard in the craft store. We laughed about a black ribbon with poodles.

The next day in class, Brother Miklaus caught me writing a note to Danny. He sent me to the office.

They locked me in the bottom of a grated wet opening, where I had to sit stewing in my hate for the weekend of endless days. Just outside the grate I could hear jackal-strangling asps shrieking all through the night. Perhaps I was hearing the sounds of my own projected anger. Almost with no sleep, but a kind of wakefulness that denies life, the body throbbed as if nails dug within. The body and I became enemies. I sweat and urinated and defecated everywhere. Phillip visited me and touched my face, for about five seconds. Then he was gone.

Finally, morning footsteps and shadows on their way to class. It was Monday. Father Percival soon unlocked me without looking or speaking. As if I were some completely terrible thing that didn't deserve to be alive. I came out absolutely filled with hate, showed up in class in sweat, dirt, piss and shit. The bathroom mirror told me that I actually looked hot, if you can believe it, but I couldn't enjoy it because it felt like eyeballs were burning in my head and my guts.

When Danny asked me for a pencil I almost threw it into his eye. Lest I do or say something to Danny or Hildegard that I would regret, at recess I went off by myself to sulk. All I could think about was Eliano, the only beautiful thing in the world. So much joy in his face when he smiles! If only he were here to comfort me in his winglike arms, everything would be ok. Walking across the football field, I saw a couple making out under the bleachers. Is it him? It couldn't be, I told myself, that would just be too ironic and cruel. Of course, it was him. And the girl was Jacqueline, a beautiful and mysterious aristocratic blonde exchange student from France. I was enraged that someone else had discovered his desirability. How could she appreciate him like I do? There's just no way.

Hildegard sat with me at lunch, very patient and loving, with no words. She knew this would be a huge relief to me, as existence felt like such a burden. It's amazing how much she actually understood me. I hate having to explain myself. Words are sometimes the ugliest thing in reality or in people's minds. Hildegard and I had such a sublime connection.

4:38 am. I saw the bloodred convertible pick Hildegard up. I was outside sitting on a stone bench with my hands in my sweatshirt pockets, shivering and knocking my knees together, having given up on sleep as usual. A tall, ageless man enveloped her in his perfect limbs, kissed her with ecstatic grace, then sealed her into the limo and sped off.

I closed my eyes and dreamed of Hildegard riding away. The driver delivered her to a mountain peak. Her slipper was the last thing that slid through the doorway. Then, the blue hand pressed her body all over until the orgasm could be heard in a scream for miles around. This being is a Christ being, therefore he is blue. He has shimmering eyelids.

The Sweating Topaz

ildegard returned a few days later. She came down with a flu, which often happened after she was away. I went into her room to check on her, and found her lying comatose, hair swirling like drugged pythons. She always needed plenty of rest after hours or days of nonstop felicity abroad.

A young barefoot apprentice came to deliver medicine from the apothecary. He gave me a vial of thick brown liquid and told me Hildegard should take it as soon as she got up.

As soon as the door shut and I put the medicine on her bedside table, Hildegard opened her eyes. "Johnny, get me my topaz, please," she said drowsily. "It's over on the vanity."

"Hildegard, you know they brought you some medicine."

"I know," she said, taking the topaz from me and placing it next to the vial. A pool of liquid started to collect around the gem, then gushed until it was dripping off the table.

"The topaz is sweating," Hildegard said. "They're trying to poison me." She didn't seem surprised. Truly a river now flowed from the table to the floor, and along a crack between floorboards. "Johnny, we have to do something."

I stared blankly.

Hildegard was able to read the patterns of dust on the windowpane, and understood that if she was not dead by morning, the priests would resort to more violent methods. But in her feverish state, she was in no position to flee.

I begged Hildegard to call on one of her otherworldly lovers to take her somewhere else, or at least to hide her until she recovered. But she only shook her head and said, "The circumstances won't allow for that now. Johnny, I leave myself in your hands. I trust you," and with a peaceful smile, she drifted back to sleep.

I freaked out for a couple hours. I tried to find Danny, but he was nowhere. I briefly considered murder/suicide with Hild as a solution. But what if Danny was right? What if there was no death? What if we ended up in a way worse predicament than we were in now?

At long last, I calmed myself the fuck down and came up with a plan.

Phillip knew a rattlesnake who had worked for the mafia. The snake was pretty rich, with tattoos, piercings, and steel teeth, among other ridiculous trends that rattlesnakes were always doing just to be cool. I thought he was just right for the job, so I hired him. I paid him with some tongues and eyeballs that I "found" in a reliquary in a shrine in a catacomb where I had often gone to bewail my pathetic, unsatisfactory life back when I was fourteen. Anyway, I had no idea what a rattlesnake would want with some shreds of a holy human being, and I was unsure whether he'd accept it. But we were desperate, I had no money, and he demanded payment upfront.

Thankfully, he snatched the relics from me without a word, as if it were any other form of currency. He slithered away like a macho asshole, without even thanking me. It didn't really bother me, his being an asshole, cause business is business and I knew he would get the job done. "But remember, leave the janitors alone and don't hurt Sister Ruth!" I must have said to him at least three times. Sister Ruth was the choir teacher—totally senile and homophobic, but a very sweet lady, definitely harmless. She was literally the only one of the teachers who showed no obvious signs of being a dangerous psychopath.

The next morning, I awoke from an anxious half-sleep beside Hildegard, to shrieks coming from the chapel. Bridget, a corny, blonde, somewhat pretty but totally annoying girl, had discovered the priests hanging in the vestry, fang marks between their ribs. They were naked. Some kids were freaking out, some were praying, others were running around lighting things on fire, and some had run away. Danny was vacillating between freaking out, praying, speculating about bizarre conspiracy theories, and coming up with incoherent schemes to escape. I tried to get him to wait with me until Hildegard recovered, and we could all run away together, but he was totally self-absorbed and impossible to communicate with. So I kind of just roamed around campus, feeling anxious and horrified. . . unfinished food with flies, trash and bodies all over. No one bothered to clean up after themselves without adult supervision. I kept nervously returning to Hildegard's room to check on her. . . I knew it was only a matter of time before word reached the Vatican, or whatever institute of power actually cares to avenge such things.

Gnarled Roots

hey came for us the next day, just as Hildegard was almost ok. She grabbed me by the wrist. "Johnny, we have to go NOW." We could hear their booming voices out in the courtyard, and the screams of everyone they were terrorizing. We had no idea what had happened to Danny, either captured, killed, or escaped. So we had to go without him. I felt horrible about leaving him there, and started running in and out of burning buildings in a last desperate effort to find him. But the stampede of flames and people almost took me down, and Hildegard pulled me away.

Hildegard and I ran into the woods. We ran in between the enormous trees of a wood so thick it obscured the penetration of sunlight. We ran for days. The days came, the nights came, the trees invisibly distant above our heads. We were safe, but we continued to run and run through the endless forest, as if through black corridors of a forgotten mansion in a deep valley untouched by the sun. We were completely possessed by the spells of witches who inhabit these woods and pass their time staging costume balls and funeral processions, and constructing luxurious palace-prisons where beings enchanted into these realms can get lost for centuries while their lives become emaciated, and others never cease forgetfully to ride carnivorous fish round and round a castle inverted in a lake, attempting to slay a sea dragon which imprisons a rag doll princess, herself bewitched to look, think, act, feel, and mourn like a real princess whose life is nothing but suffering.

Hildegard and I ran through these woods, ourselves reduced to bandits in black rags clutching our short knives and the change purses of petty kings we ambushed on the roads, in our hasty escape into hiding. I've never felt this kind longing for Hildegard. I may even want to fuck her. She glanced at me from time to time with love shining in her dark eyes as we ran, now tripping over thick gnarled roots up to our knees.

We slowed our pace, as the network of roots beneath our feet became too obstructive. Or because time has become eclipsed. How long have we been running? Twilight now exists. The air was full of the smell of lilacs and white moths' wings. Our destination became apparent: before us, emerging from tree roots, stood a castle of gray polished stone veined with pink and pale red, turrets that slashed victoriously into the sky, windowpanes and shutters glinting like teeth of welcome.

We crept through thick vines and all kinds of grandiose flowers and horned insects. These gardens were clearly not kept by humans, they were too wild and fantastic. Cautiously, we approached the huge panels of translucent marble which formed the front gate, along flagstones overgrown with blades of grass shooting above our heads.

A pretty girl whose eyes, hair and skin were all tan and shone with delight, came out to greet us. She led us inside.

A flaming pentagram rosette window threw fearsome rainbows in many directions, onto the ivory marble banisters, amethyst floor, and noble ornaments arching from the walls. Behind every window, courtyards beckoned.

The girl led us to a dressing chamber where we could remove our filthy black bandits' rags and change into the outfits of our choice. We both selected matching worn black shreds, identical to the ones we had been wearing, but smelling faintly of frankincense instead of mud and sweat.

The girl told us we were free to explore the place, and dinner would be served after the sun had set seven degrees below the ground. Then she disappeared behind a velvet curtain of wondrous length.

It seemed like no one else was there. The silence in this place made me restless, so I just followed Hildegard around. We got lost several times in garden hedge mazes that, from inside, appeared like fish intestines. The sun was soon setting and the air was cold, with occasional moths the size of human heads gliding by. We spotted a superb-looking humanoid creature at a distance, disappearing just beyond sight with a long red train trailing behind.

The Princes of
A Million Pines

inner was such a tempest, I can scarcely remember anything. All I can recall is hundreds of people running through a grand gilded hall that seemed to stretch on forever, screaming. Hildegard and I quickly lost one another. She was swept up ahead of me, in a group of bald, shrieking females. Skies and trees and torchlight blurred through the windows, as joy and trampling echoes vanquished my thoughts. As if the hall were swallowing and digesting living beings. This continued for hours, Hildegard and I and our new companions chasing our lives away.

From the corner of my vision, several times through the crowd, I noticed two fantastic young gentlemen eying me with curiosity. They were seated on a citrine and gold velvet loveseat along an open window in a recessed corner, where star jasmine overflowed from outside. The boy wearing pinstriped white had blonde eyes and silver hair. Or was it light yellow? I was so dazzled by his appearance, I frankly couldn't tell you. His crown perched among his locks like a gilt swan brandishing a variety of pearlescent twigs. The other boy had eyes black as space and a pride-destroying grin. His crown was so golden it was violent. He placed his fingers under my chin and asked me something cryptic.

Attempting to answer him, I mumbled something incomprehensible. The boys' laughter overthrew me like a torrent of flowers, and I toppled over. I landed sprawled across them, and we struck up a conversation. The blonde was called Josh and the black-eyed one was Arcady. I soon learned that these were the elf princes of a shadowy realm called A Million Pines.

To an ordinary visitor lacking in fortune, A Million Pines is an abandoned off-season ski town in the Summer. Wind and rustling pine needles are the only sounds in the empty streets.

"Oh please tell me more about A Million Pines!" I begged. Josh firmed his grip on my calf and Arcady twisted a lock of my hair. Then they simultaneously burst into song, a haunting yet agreeable folk tune. I was shocked to hear Josh sing in such a spirited way, for he seemed so shy and quiet. Arcady shouted dramatically and gave my chest a jiggle every time they came to the words A MILLION PINES.

When newlyweds
get lost on their honeymoons
and miss their destinations
and drive off crumbling cliffs,
they chance across
A MILLION PINES

When cunning children
sneak out at night
to live the secret lives
they HUNGER for
they chance upon
A MILLION PINES

Our catacombs house
not bones (NOT BONES)
but incorrupt'ble bodies
of Saints who've mastered death.

Those countless arrows
of the clocks
of the tow'rs
of A MILLION PINES
swing in all directions.
But not a single soul in all a
MILLION PINES
spares a single care for
such a wretched thing as time.

I couldn't tell if this was like an A Million Pines national anthem, a popular drinking song, or an embarrassingly cliché folk song that young people liked to mock.

Josh and Arcady were guests in this castle, just like Hildegard and me. Over the next few days I became quite close to them. We would go walking in the gardens after lunch to gaze at the flowers which took flight around the garden like errant bats, and we got to know one another. Josh was quiet and gentle, very philosophical and occult. His smile was truly a cause for great rapture. Arcady was a bit feisty and self-indulgent, with a faithful heart.

Josh would get up hours before sunrise and disappear into the mountains. Arcady liked to sleep in till about noon, when the sunlight was streaming through the windows, and their 1800-thread-count sheets were quite thrashed about and dragging on the floor. But at night, after everyone had gone to bed and I still suffered mightily from the insomnia that had afflicted me back home, Arcady would draw me into a septagonal parlour in the Northern tower's library and cradle me on the great green divan by the fireplace. We would drowsily chatter and flip through art books, or he would read to me from one of the library's ancient illuminated manuscripts. When he read to me, Arcady couldn't help himself from throwing in fantastic details until the whole thing had degraded into a horror story of some kind, and he would toss the book onto the floor and keep talking until I fell asleep in his arms. He'd eventually fall asleep there with me, as the fire burnt out.

Then, just as my eyes opened to the black morning cold, Josh would show up to see if I wanted to join him on his morning excursion. He'd take me through secret tunnels in the mountains, or swimming in ice-cold rivers under waterfalls. My skin and organs felt like they were going to shatter from the cold, and Josh captured my body again and again underneath the water. Then we would stare at the rising sun until it burned incomprehensible bliss into our hearts and bodies.

At the castle, usually there'd be some skits or a short play or something in the evenings. Sometimes they were really amazing, with over-the-top costumes and really wicked, stylized dialogue—like when Evan and Leonor co-wrote and directed *The Failed Martyrdom of Bertrand Flor of Little Dublintown*. And Hildegard was able to get together a group of 72 maidens of Celestine lineage for the Greek choir, which spectacularly dematerialized between acts. But just as often, the shows were simply bad. Don't get me wrong, I'm totally into bad theater, but these were unwatchably bad, cliché, not even bad enough to be funny, boring, melodramatic, with lugubrious cellos and basses drawling away during the painfully long pauses in dialogue.

One such night, Arcady whisked me away to the tower, where we spent hours talking and laughing. Then he tucked me in with a tale.

Once there was a pair of gorgeous lovers who lived in a volcanic palace of wonder in a prosperous land. They passed each day and night in leisure, and life soon became a bore. So the lovers visited the Archangel Metatron and asked to be his disciples. They wished to learn occult techniques to manipulate reality and make life more fun.

Since the lovers were able to offer Metatron human-size models of all 13 Archimedean solids in solid rose gold, the Archangel accepted them as disciples. Under his guidance, the lovers trained diligently until they showed signs of success: one could fly and walk through mountains, and the other could transform himself into fire, control the minds of animals, and so forth. The lovers freed all their indentured servants, for now marvelous self-created attendants brought them whatever they wished, without ever needing to be asked. They would often go out cavorting together, riding on leopards, or perched between the wings of gigantic condors. The loving bond between them became so strong, it would usually cause their bodies to melt into liquid light during sex.

Their bodies knew no limitations, and they surrounded each other always with many emanated bodies, each one more charming than the next, so that their satisfaction only increased in each moment.

Soon this new life became as boring and predictable as the last. Nothing ever seemed to happen anymore. One lover wandered into the mountains to live quietly in contemplation. The other set about committing all sorts of forbidden actions he had never even thought of doing before—looting the towns, robbing and murdering, raping people, and other acts too outrageous to even name.

After a few years passed, one had become a fully accomplished mystic living in the mountains; the other had become a great psychopathic evil outlaw, living in luxurious hiding with all his hoarded wealth and prisoners.

One day they met by chance at a crossroads on the outskirts of the town, and were perplexed as they reflected on how their lives had taken such different directions. They decided to once again approach the Archangel Metatron, to ask him about this.

When the Archangel heard what had happened, he chastised the psychopathic student, who then flew into a rage and killed his teacher, then killed his ex-lover, their blood and entrails trailing behind wherever he went.

Back in his lair, the outlaw developed such one-pointed aimless rage, he became the best psychopathic evil outlaw in the world. He was terrifying to look at, with large, mad eyes and wild hair, a muscular body, and arms and legs that moved around too fiendishly and too quickly. He devoured everything in sight and sailed through oceans of the blood of his victims. At first he consumed only living things, humans, tigers, insects, trees, etc.; then, when no more living beings remained, he began to eat dirt, rocks, glass shards, cigarette butts, crumbly hamburger buns that had been sitting on a shelf for hundreds of years, cities, worlds, and universes. He washed it all down by guzzling the entire ocean of suffering that lapped at the shore of the realm. Still, the monster's eyes were enflamed with craving.

Meanwhile, in the paradisiac land where his teacher and ex-lover had wound up after being murdered, the good disciple watched his old companion with chagrin in his master's magic mirror. They decided they would have to do something, and save the confused beast from his own destructive habits.

So, the Archangel and the good disciple rode to the monster's wilderness on a dragon with nine epithets, pierced the monster's heart with a sword of a nine blades, and after the monster wept nine tears of blood from his heart, each as large as nine oceans and containing nine thorns from nine nine-petaled roses, the monster naturally agreed to give up his evil ways. And all the archangels of heaven and earth rejoiced.

The reunited lovers made a pact to stay together forever, healing all beings. Metatron blessed them and returned to his heaven. The lovers changed into a pair of doves and returned to the earthly realm, where they forgot who they were and lived out their lives simply, flitting from tree to tree, in harmony. Nobody knows what happened to the doves after that. Perhaps they became lost in the ocean of the world's joy and suffering?

By the time Arcady finished his tale, I was comfortably asleep in his arms. His voice was so melodious that even the fiercest, most terrifying words would drip over me ambrosially and soothe all hungers and lack. Those were the best nights of sleep I'd ever known.

As usual, I woke up hours before dawn, and Josh immediately cracked open the door to take me out with him. We were early enough, so we went out to wait in the usual spot for Josh's familiar, a wild stag, to fetch us. We galloped at a frightening pace through the forest, along the river, across an abyss, and up a mountain of sharp crags to await the sun exploding into our eyes.

"I honestly have no idea how to get to this spot on my own," Josh told me the first time we did this together. He had tried many times, but had to give up for sheer confusion. Only through the grace of the familiar can so many things become possible!

On the way back, in the midst of some chasm or another, Hildegard rode past us on her white ceffyl dŵr and passed me a fortune cookie. I crunched on it and Josh and I read the fortune together and laughed, as it made no sense at all. Just like life, y'know?

"Have you ever been hunting, Johann?" Josh asked me one evening.

I told him no, of course not. Hunting is something I've always associated with aristocratic assholes.

"I'm going to take you out hunting tomorrow."

"What? I thought you were vegan." I really hadn't seen him eat anything at all, except on high feast days, and then just little salads of leaves and dew drops and ceremonial cakes of acorn pulp, berries and sweet chestnut butter.

"Well, mostly vegan, I guess, " he said. Then the unreal smile and laugh like the breaking of twigs.

He brought me to a strange wood I'd never been to before. The trees grew in spirals, and the clouds moved in spirals, and I could see golden stars twinkling in the sky, though it was broad daylight. Josh seemed to know where he was going, though there were no trails. We hardly talked at all, but he kept turning to look at me, which I could never get enough of. He'd give me that laugh and smile, whose complete wholesome beauty destroys my sense of peace any time I think of it.

In this wild wood the trees were very broad and climbed out of the ground at unusual angles as if made of wax and dripping with sap that smelled like sandalwood and burnt sugar.

At some length of time, impossible to determine, we arrived at a meadow. Josh knelt on the long grass, and I sat down next to him. He took his spearhead, pierced his left palm, and squeezed out a perfect drop of blood. Then he bowed his head and waited. I was forced to stare silently at the ecstatic shape of Josh's bowing neck and those vertebrae poking out the back, which caused me to feel slightly crazed. But I didn't dare touch him now, when he was really concentrating.

Suddenly a creature came running happily out of the woods, a baby wild boar, and began to lick the blood on Josh's hand. Josh pet the little beast, who bowed his head to the ground, then rolled over on his back, his four legs wide open and his underside vulnerable. Then the little thing closed his eyes and died, at which point Josh took his spear and cut out the boar's heart cleanly in three cuts.

"I'm not stricly vegan," said Josh, as we shared the sweet heart meat, "but I only eat meat when it's offered to me freely." The pink blood dribbled down his chin.

The Enchanted
Dalmation

osh, Arcady and I were lying in a heap in the Northern tower, on a bed whose walnut posts were pairs of entwined snakes reaching to the ceiling. I couldn't really relax because of the choir's unworldly banshee-like wails coming from the chapel. I mean, I can't say it wasn't beautiful, but it had been going on for about 13 hours. Hildegard had no regard for anything when the choir was on a role. Arcady was sleeping in the crook of my arm, pulling my hand towards his throat. "How did you and Arcady meet, anyway?" I asked Josh. I figured it would be a boring story, that they had both come from royal elf families somewhere, etc. But I felt like listening to Josh talk, and he didn't talk very much unless prompted. Josh told me the story.

"When I was 15, my parents sent me to summer camp. (My parents worked for the Swiss embassy and they wanted me to learn how to dwell among humans.) That summer was very lonely for me. I had no friends and I felt unable to relate to humans. My counselor was a beefy airhead and I had nothing to say to anyone. My only real friend at camp was this dalmation who usually hung around the swimming pool. He was called Muffin. We were pals. He'd come bounding up to me whenever he saw me, and it always perked me up. I'd kneel down and scratch his cute head as his tongue lolled around and licked my face. 'Muffin,' I'd say to him, 'you're a good guy. Thanks for hanging out with me.'

"Well, I kept telling myself that things would get better at camp, I just had to meet my peeps. By the third week, I did have one friend, this gothic girl named Mallory Duchess. We bonded one night in the arts and crafts studio, when I expressed admiration for the geometric sculpture of a pig crowned with belladonna that she was working on. But every day, I would look forward above all to seeing my dear Muffin, who was always there for me and always accepted me no matter what.

"One hot, humid afternoon, I was sitting out by the pool in a chaise lounge with Muffin in my lap. The other kids were playing water polo and I was pretending to have a stomach ache because I hated being in loud, crowded pools. I much preferred the lake back home, surrounded by emerald mountain peaks, where you can dive and dive for miles as all of existence dissolves into the dark with stars, colored lights and tunnels leading to underwater cities built by extinct races. Anyway, after the water polo game was over, I told my counselor I'd catch up with them in a few minutes. The truth was I needed some peace and quiet.

After everyone had gone, and I was sitting there watching the afternoon sunlight glinting off the surface of the swimming pool, I kissed my little Muffin right between the eyes. Immediately he sprang into the shape of my beloved Arcady! He'd been enchanted into a dog form and had been living that way for a few years. Apparently all he needed was a kiss between the eyes from another elf prince to break the spell. We've been together ever since."

What a wonderful way to find true love, I thought. Wouldn't it be nice if I could find my true dæmon lover? I wish it were so easy.

An Emerald Summer

ne day I put a spoonful of Arcady's porridge into my mouth and it was different. More rich and sophisticated, somehow. I figured he must be in one of his moods—those extravagant moods which I knew so well. Arcady would go into town and spend several hundred thousand dollars on a new crown, or a diamond-encrusted brioche, or a lake of burning lilies in the Italian Alps. Sometimes he would just go to fancy department stores and try on suits or completely impractical ceremonial garb, stuff he would never actually buy or wear, and look at himself in the mirror. I went with him once. It was amazing the way the shop girls all responded to him. I was kind of bored, but he bought me a gilded parasol with silk flowers on it. Anyway,

the porridge was thick, black and sweet. On first bite it tasted delicious, spiced with star anise, thyme and saffron in excessive amounts. What a princely porridge! But it was kind of sick after a few bites, it was so rich. When Arcady got into these moods, he'd slather way too much saffron on everything. Do you know how expensive saffron is? It was obvious he had grown up a spoiled prince and never known anything resembling lack. I could really only eat a few bites of that porridge.

Arcady spent hours playing video games. Mostly first-person shooters and action-adventure games. Sometimes he would go a couple days without even going outside. On the most exquisite summer day he'd be sitting there in his darkened room, a steaming clay pot of porridge among old obscure history books and avant-garde men's fashion magazines where all the models looked androgynous, lovelorn and orphaned far away from their homeland, with his new crown crooked on his head, scattering light chaotically from the video game screen. His fighting character was called Nomenclate, a warrior-ambassador from Crete. His mission was to deliver an envelope which contained an important document to a political figure in Rome, a member of the secret government. I tried the game once, but I didn't really get it. Still, for some reason I liked to sit there and watch him play. This had become my favorite place in the whole castle for relaxing whenever I felt overwhelmed—right next to Arcady with his video game blaring on. I'm not an adult, I have no idea what to do with myself sometimes.

A knock at the door.

Hildegard brought us cupcakes made of mung beans with turmeric and topped with coconut, golden berries, and red antioxidant fruit powder. With the dark evil taste of that porridge still sticking to my mouth, the cupcakes were so mild and divine.

"Is that a new crown?" Hildegard asked Arcady.

"Yes, babe, I was feeling a bit spunky yesterday, so I went to the mall to try on clothes," he answered without turning to look at her from the screen.

"I told the guy I was invited to a fancy brunch in August, and he let me try on whatever I wanted. Then I found this baby here and rescued it on a whim."

"Are those pearls and garnets set in brass?" Hildegard looked horrified.

"Yes, isn't it lovely," answered Arcady, ignoring her tone and with his eyes still fixed on the monitor.

Hildegard was obviously considering whether or not she should start lecturing him. "You know, brass is a very hot metal, completely impure and unnatural and has no virtue. It's going to attract illness. And garnet is a lovely stone, but I wouldn't go about wearing it casually all day like that... it develops during a lunar eclipse, making it wonderful for certain activities, but if you wear it too long it will penetrate your whole body and dry it up. And where there are garnets, the airy spirits are unable to bring their phantasms to completion! No wonder you sit around playing video games all day long." She waved her arms around irritably, but Arcady just rolled his eyes and ignored her. He had come to a pivotal moment in his game, and started vigorously manipulating the controller.

"Why can't you get a simple gold or platinum crown set with diamonds and topaz? Talk some sense into him, Johnny!"

I felt mentally slow and entranced whenever I sat on Arcady's bed with him, watching him play his video games. "What?" I asked Hildegard dumbly.

"Oh, nevermind!" she said, and briskly left the room.

That was the summer that Hildegard became obsessed with the color green. She sewed emeralds into everything she owned, and every day she wore the emerald headdress that the castle traditionally reserved for St. Cecilia's feast day. Hildegard would just lounge around in socks, pajamas, and that headdress. She convinced some of the artists who were good at working with marble to build a large white marble pyramid in a certain location, since she said that the pyramid is the shape that attracts green light. They built a perfect pyramid there, with charming relief carvings of people flying around and relaxing at the beach. I never saw green light around that pyramid, so I don't know if she was talking metaphorically or just making shit up, but I know at certain times that summer, some of us definitely saw bright green light flying out of her body. And for about 5 days straight her body was actually green. Arcady says he even saw her emerald skeleton during one of those nights.

Arcady was up in the clock tower with her, as it was pouring warm rain and lightning, one of our fabulous summer storms. The tower had open windows and rain was flying in and out. Arcady was just lying down on the wet couch in the dark, and Hildegard was sobbing, trembling, and trying to transcribe poetry from angels at the same time. So Arcady offered to have her dictate to him and he'd write it down. She grabbed a short sword off the wall and swiftly hacked off her arm, catching the severed end and holding it up to him like a torch. The bones were bright green, transparent and glowing. Of course, Hildegard reattached her arm with no problem, once Arcady had faithfully completed his transcription.

Hildegard also laughed a lot during that period, as if drunk. And when she looked at me it was frightening. I didn't know what that look meant. Was she about to say something? Was she mad at me? Did she want something from me? Did she want to jump my bones? She held my gaze inappropriately long and I got really uncomfortable. Was she spacing out, did she even know I was there? Others noticed that weird moment too and then we all laughed about it and went for a swim.

The entire castle found itself most enriched by all this green everywhere, which Hildegard said was the most life-giving, healing color and the true color of sunlight. She fasted on spirulina and said the quickest way to transform one's mind was to eat exclusively green foods. I overheard her repeating this to other people more than once.

Hildegard was growing a little parsley in the corner of the herb garden, and her prayers caused it to grow, covering the castle in a big, tight, wet green web. People had difficulty opening windows and had to break through the tough branches of parsley. By the end of the day, the parsley was starting to grow inside the castle and by the end of the week, covering all the walls on the inside as well. This parsley miraculously had no apparent need for light to survive, as I never once saw any leaves wilt or show signs of decline. Just occasional broken stems from where someone had grabbed a clump as a refreshing afternoon snack. Hildegard recommended parsley as a perfect antidote to the morbid thoughts that tend to arise during the devil's hour.

One day, about 6 months later, long after Hildegard had gotten over her obsession with green, the parsley just sort of crumbled to fine dust and disintegrated when touched. Within a week there was no sign of it.

My mind would drift sometimes to Danny. What had happened to him? Had he managed to escape? Every so often I would mail letters to any distant provinces I could think of, trying to find him. But I never heard back. I missed him, even his zealous vendetta against God. That boy hated God obsessively.

No one here at the castle ever talked about God. Hildegard still prayed all the time, and the seven divine hours were always observed each day in the chapel, but I never went. Once I asked Hildegard if God really existed. She just cackled alarmingly, and got that ecstatic look in her eye, and I left it at that. Danny was so convinced that God not only existed, but was the most horrible thing in the world. In the peaceful, boring moments at the castle, I sometimes would wonder.

Part II

The Love of God

od created Adam and Lilith. Since God was a man, Adam was his favorite. Since God was gay, He and Adam were lovers. That's actually why God created Adam in the first place. God was gay and lonely, and had no one to cuddle with and go prancing with through the meadows of His creation. So God created Adam in His own image, so that Adam would be worthy of His love.

When God sculpted Adam out of the mud of the earth, He breathed life into him. When God saw what He had made, He was very turned on. God and Adam became twins and frolicked each day in the valleys and hills of Eden, hiking to the tops of wild plateaus and making love beneath the crystal clear blue skies with the sunlight beating down on their bare asses. God and Adam's love life resembled a Western-style porn movie.

The reason God was gay was because His mother had mishandled his sensitive needs as an infant. His mother, the howling black she-wolf of oblivion, would smother him with affection at times, and completely ignore him at other times. That's how God developed an aversion to females and became a gay man.

At the very instant God created Adam, Lilith was inadvertently born of God's fear and sexual desire's shadow, which no human being can possibly face, and hope to remain sane.

As much as one might try all one's life to forget one's mother and one's past, one cannot escape history. One's roots always come back to haunt one, and for God it was no different. For God is One. Lilith was born out of God's unwillingness to deal with his intimacy issues.

She lurked around mostly at night, otherwise retreating to unknown areas. God pretended not to notice her and courted Adam as if nothing were awry, but whenever he caught a glimpse of Lilith, God felt sick.

Ever since creating Adam, God had been finally enjoying life. He had someone to love and care for, and Adam was an excellent boyfriend, always picking him wondrous flowers, giving him massages, and whispering lovingly in his ear as they lay by the fire at night. God took Adam to secret caves and fed him ambrosia from ancient pools. They ran around the forest with erections, and made out in trees. God and Adam really took care of each other.

Then one day, something very sad happened. In the cold half-light of dawn, Adam suddenly woke up. God was still asleep. Adam heard a rustling of twigs, and turned in the direction of the sound. He saw, outlined against the black earth and tree trunks and a white dawn sky, a human figure.

Up until that time, Adam had never met another human besides God. Now he saw a mysterious third figure with an unknown body.

Lilith's body frightened and totally captivated Adam. She loomed like an effortless, majestic chasm/charm. He wanted her.

Adam hesitated a moment and turned to God, who was still sleeping. Then the kid unwrapped himself from God's arms and ran after Lilith, the unknown being.

Lilith smiled and darted away. She led Adam through the fog, over hills and into forests, in and out of babbling streams and through caverns.

Each time he nearly caught up with her, Lilith would laugh and lightly spring off again. Adam had to continually stop to catch his breath, happy and salivating like a horny dog. But he never lost spirit. Finally, after a few hours of this sport, Lilith allowed the boy to catch her in a bed of honeysuckles and they tumbled around together gleefully.

Adam fell madly in love with Lilith. God was pissed and hurt.

God became obsessed with sorrow and began to hate his creation. He started to think about death, sickness, pain and ugliness, concepts which had never occurred to him before. He started getting some wild ideas.

God retreated to a tiny mountain cottage with moldy walls and blood-orange stained glass windows caked with dirt. A fire raged in the fireplace all through the hot summer days, making a hideous squealing sound and filling the cottage with thick black smoke. God's hair turned white and he grew a long white beard to which clung particles of ash and smoke. He coughed and hacked and studied ancient incomprehensible alchemical texts at his desk in the study, not caring about anything. Adam was long gone, probably out enjoying the marvels of existence with the cursèd vixen, and God was all alone and outcast.

One day, God was sitting at his antique mahogany desk, contemplating a disorganized diagram in one of his alchemical tomes. He peered out the window and spied Adam and Lilith skipping along out on the grassy hill. Their naked faces beamed bright. God had somehow forgotten how fucking cute Adam had been and was senseless with jealousy and heartbreak. That was it.

God stormed out of His shack and ran after Adam and Lilith with a pitchfork. He caught up with them as they were stupidly tumbling around the burned-out, picturesque ruins of a brick house at the edge of a wood.

"You!" God barked, startling them. Adam didn't recognize God at first, but Lilith felt icy dread, for she knew exactly who He was. God pointed His pitchfork at Lilith, His enemy, the one part of His creation that had been unforeseen and spited Him. He opened his mouth and a caterwauling spell forced its way out. Lightening bolts shot out of His pitchfork and struck Lilith's body, breaking her bones. Her head turned leather-black and her skin all fried, fangs and slits for eyes, with a black and white checkerboard pattern on her back. Smiling evilly, Lilith stuck out her forked tongue, whipped the air with her tail, and bolted off into the forest.

Adam's face turned gray and rubbery. His eyes and skin lost their marvelous luster almost instantly, and then he began to wail. Sobs exploded out of his throat and tears and mucus poured. God stood aghast as He realized what He had done. He started to approach Adam, wanting nothing more than to comfort him. Adam curled up in a ball on the grass and God put His hands on the boy's back and stroked his head, but Adam took no comfort in this. He continued to sob violently and beat the ground with his hands. He was so consumed by grief that he did nothing but roll around catatonically all day long.

Meanwhile, God retreated back to His shack, which was now a tower of darkness. Every moment was full of mourning. Where God glanced, dirty icicles appeared, cracked and fell to bits. He thought more about death and deterioration. He thought about endings and became obsessed with nonexistence. He sealed himself in the top room of His tower and started to madly type away on his laptop, writing tragic endings to stories that had never begun. He typed so viciously the keyboard started to break. As He continued typing His story, He would pause to rip keys off His keyboard, one by one, and His writing became more and more jumbled. Eventually, all the keys were gone except the Esc key, which God banged on as hard as He could over and over again. He couldn't block out the sound of Adam screaming for Lilith.

"Bring her back! Give her back! I need her! She's the only thing! Bring her back to me, or invent Death so that I can leave this place forever!" Adam was lying in a gutter somewhere screaming and God could hear him all the while from His tower of darkness, because God was clairaudient.

After finally ripping off the Esc key and then throwing the entire laptop out the highest window in His tower, God lay down on the stone floor for 45 minutes feeling sorry for Himself. Then He took a good honest look at His life. This was ridiculous. He got up off the floor and walked down His long spiral staircase and out the door. He jumped on his bike and pedaled away across the hills and meadows to where Adam was crouching in the gutter, beating his fist against the slimy concrete. As he heard God's footsteps,

Adam turned to see Him, who once again looked like a cute hunk with wavy red-brown hair.

God reached his hand down to Adam. Adam feebly took the hand and let God help him up.

"Bbbbbring her back," Adam whined, getting snot all over God's shoulder.

"I can't do that. I hate her."

Adam was silent.

God tried all sorts of tricks to get Adam back. He tried ignoring, begging, flirting, shaming, comforting, etc., but nothing worked. God realized that this wasn't the same perfect, faithful boyfriend that He had created. Damn it, how created things change! God lamented the treacherous nature of His creation. Adam was his own person now, with his own feelings and desires. He was no longer in love with his creator.

God grew his hair a little longer so it was shaggy and fashionably unkempt. He took long walks by Himself in the fog. He visited Adam once in a while, but it was like visiting an old relative who doesn't have a life anymore. Depressing.

Soon it became apparent that of the two of them, Adam was doing much worse. He couldn't even keep himself together in the most basic of ways. At least God was changing his clothing daily and going on walks. Adam just lay around. God realized He didn't even really find Adam attractive anymore, and stopped visiting him.

Adam started showing up at God's house every day, wearing the same dirty hoody with dried toothpaste spit and dandruff all over it. He was still sort of cute, but his face and shoulders were all droopy. Eventually God felt sorry for the guy and let him in. Adam would just sprawl on the couch, watch really bad daytime soap operas with the volume too loud, and ask God to make him a sandwich. This went on for days.

Soon God felt sure He would vomit and go crazy if He had to bear that depressing eyesore in His living room one more moment. And for the first time, God felt genuine compassion for someone other than Himself. By some inexplicable miracle, even though He knew He would be bitter and depressed forever about Adam's betrayal, God made a very selfless decision. It made no sense for both of them to be miserable.

God crept up to Adam and took him by the arm. He helped him off the couch and laid him down on the rug in front of the fireplace. God picked up a butter knife that Adam had discarded on the living room floor after buttering a piece of toast a week ago. The knife was still studded with tiny dry crumbs stuck to a fine film of butter.

"It'll only hurt for a moment," God said, as He stuck the knife in Adam's side and began to saw off one of Adam's ribs. Adam grimaced and moaned a bit, but he was still semi-catatonic and his senses were dull.

For a moment God breathed in the nostalgic smell of Adam's flannel, which filled Him with longing for their unlived life together. Then He popped out the boy's rib and cried a single tear onto it. He placed it on the floor, and...voila. Eve sprang to life. She was pretty and well-mannered, with pink lipstick and big, blue eyes. Of course she was totally annoying, but Adam adored her right away, and they ambled away together arm in arm, leaving God alone in His tower.

Loneliness Breeds in the Heart of the Vile Womyn

ilith was a voluptuous woman, almost fat. She had waist-length black hair that glared blue in the sun, and eyes the color of blue computer screens with black flecks. Lilith was forty years old, but looked about fourteen. Actually, she was thousands of years old, as old as human consciousness, and perhaps even older than that. But she liked to think of herself as forty.

Lilith lived in a castle of black spires on a still lake. In the forest, which is silent by day, with rustling twigs, and where by night the vague shrieks of the trees can be heard. A curious forest which promises to grant all wishes, making one feel most uneasy. Lilith lived alone.

Long ago, hundreds of years ago, the castle had housed an entire court. Children laughed in the courtyards, maids gossiped in the kitchens, and pages whistled in the corridors. For hundreds of years, Lilith had held court, handsomely entertaining visitors from all over the universe.

Amor Lucindo, one of Arcady's more illustrious ancestors, had often visited. He had been known to spend hours with Lilith in her boudoir high up in the Eastern tower. Hysterical laughter was always heard from that window whenever Amor Lucindo was in town. Lilith's diary was full of retellings of Amor Lucindo's baffling stories of his travels abroad, like the time when an entire caravan of gypsies had captured him and force-fed him strawberry cakes until he'd turned tepid yellow and acted like a fly, or when he was continually interrupted in a speech he was giving to the New Grecian Council of Lebanon by an adorable young princess who wanted to ask his opinion on her shoes.

Lilith's household of attendants, maids and pages had continually sung her praises, as she took excellent care of all their desires and needs, and she was generally loved by everyone around her. She also took excellent care of herself through diet, lifestyle, spiritual practices, etc. For three years, Lilith ate nothing but carrots, wheat grass juice and brown rice protein powder as an experiment, and felt terrific.

"The sons of Israel are so hot," said Lilith casually to God one day. "Probably the only thing that could stop me from seducing and fucking every last one of them is for someone to cut their cock hoods off!" She laughed like it was a joke, but the sorceress knew just how God's paranoid mind worked.

God ruminated about Lilith's "joke" for the rest of the day. *Was it just a twisted joke? Was she serious? Was she messing with me? Am I being too uptight? Maybe I just need to relax and not take life so seriously. But I do need to protect My beloved people from that fucking demoness.* God finally strategized that the best course of action would be to bully the Israelites into sexually mutilating their male infants.

God told Abraham to take his son, Isaac, up to a barren mountain at dawn and sacrifice the boy as an offering. Abraham, who was not actually a psychopathic idiot, just a normal God-fearing guy paralyzed with terror, got his knife all ready. Isaac was so cute. Abraham was just about to go in for the stab, but at the last minute God sent His angel to interrupt them.

"JUST KIDDING!" God and the angel started laughing maniacally. Abraham and Isaac joined in, because sometimes you just have to play along with your abuser for your own safety.

Then when the laughter died down, God got serious again. "Because I Love you and all the Children of Israel, this will symbolize our Love," said God. "There has to be blood, and it has to leave a scar. Otherwise how will I know you love me?"

Since God was so freaky and terrifying, Abraham obeyed and then convinced all his friends and everyone he knew to similarly sexually mutilate their male children.

Lilith's servant girls waded through the Israelites' trash, collecting foreskin. Then Lilith laughed all the way to her friend Dr. Steinberg's skincare lab in Switzerland, where the doctor used all the foreskins to make a truly phenomenal lotion that Lilith made all her attendants use. She hated it when one of her servants was adjusting her bonnet, and grazed her neck with the back of a hand that was just average.

One day, in the year 666, Lilith got bored with life. She found no meaning in anything anymore.

All she did all day was dine, take long candlelit baths, have sex, and go hunting for golden stags with the most cunning and fascinating men of the day. Nothing seemed to really matter, and Lilith was suddenly faced with the abysmal meaninglessness of existence. She stopped inviting people over. She stopped speaking. She sat in a sumptuous throne with velvet cushions, which was now no more to her than a mockery of anything good in life. She was wearing a brilliant vermillion dress and jeweled tiara, gloves and hat, and she didn't even bother changing into something more somber, such were the depths of her apathy. She sat in the corner of her parlor and gazed out the window at the doves, which flew in and out by day, and the bats that screeched by at night. She resolved to sit on that throne until she died, if that were possible.

Day by day, all Lilith's guests, attendants, mascots, and so on, the entire court, abandoned her until she was utterly alone in her castle.

She sat on that throne for years and decades and centuries. She would sit on that throne until the day she died, and if that day never came, Lilith was prepared to sit on that throne forever.

The forest became a dangerous place. Vultures flew by her window and craned their necks to peek inside at the sorceress, who had become a curiosity in the land. Vipers played about in the overgrown courtyard and made love in broad daylight.

Lilith continued to sit. The dress she wore, originally the color of burning leaves and fire, became tattered with the muck of the ages. Her diamonds turned brown and cracked. The hat began to disintegrate into an absurd floppy puzzlement. But despite her resolve to die, Lilith's body remained vital and true. The body that she no longer cared about, for life held no more meaning for her than death.

Lilith's mind wandered here and there, sometimes blank, sometimes distracted with insignificant memories. Each time it occurred to her, Lilith renewed her resolve to sit on that throne until her end.

Then, one day, on a whim, Lilith changed her mind.

She got up, ripped off her clothes, took a shower and changed into a red and black silk bathrobe that looked like a kimono. This was the beginning of a new life.

Lilith moved to Ireland. She bought a fortress called Dubhcolm Castle, from a dwindling family of bankrupt and schizophrenic aristocrats who had been living half in decaying luxury, half in filth for several years. They had fought to hold on to every last emblem of their former wealth and status, and Dubhcolm was the last to go.

O Dubhcolm Castle
on a lake
on emerald pastures
near the open sea.
How lovely
How charming
O,
Dear Dubhcolm Castle

Lilith burned all the furniture and polished all the stones, to get rid of the former owners' grime. She spent the nights filling the empty stone towers with her howling, and the days strolling and dancing around the countryside. The townspeople began to catch glimpses of their new neighbor combing her hair with an ivory comb while perched on the rugged stones, or in flowing black dresses, milking black cows in the pastures. Soon word of this mysterious young girl reached the king.

The Grand Marquis of Hell

ing Damon was a voracious warrior, and would ordinarily put an end to any other powerful individuals that appeared in the neighborhood. He sent his soldiers to surround Dubhcolm, but Lilith turned them to dust with a glance. So he brought down a storm of vultures on the place, but Lilith speared and roasted every last one of them in her moat of fire for a banquet. So the king sent billions of diseased toads to bring Lilith to ruin; but she made them her lovers, then carved them up and sewed their skins together into a long, elegant shawl, which draped behind her many fathoms as she promenaded through the countryside.

Meanwhile, Princess Dymphna, the king's only child, had been sneaking out to spy on

Lilith. The fourteen-year-old princess had lost her mother to St. Anthony's fire a year before, and longed for companionship. Dymphna was bored and lonely, and frankly sick of her creepy dad. And when she saw how marvelously Lilith showed her dominion, the princess fell instantly in love. She convinced her father that he would need the sorceress as an ally. Then the girl left a wreath of lilies on Lilith's doorstep, as a token of peace from the king.

Lilith and Dymphna became the best of friends. They languished away many a fine spring afternoon in the princess's bedroom, doing each other's hair, singing and playing music together, and summoning spirits for their amusement.

One endless May evening, fragrant with jasmine and monotonous with the twinkling of stars and candlelight, the girls decided to summon Phenex, a Grand Marquis of Hell, to help them with their poetry. Dymphna was trying to convey in verse the feeling of being freed from the bonds of flesh by the virile stroke of a lover in the form of a bolt of lightning, and she had hit an impasse in her writing.

Phenex, who had a child's voice and lavender velvet breeches and waistcoat, waltzed into the princess's bedroom surrounded by masses of his demons in attendance. The Marquis commanded 20 legions of demons, who formed his entourage and accompanied him everywhere.

Phenex told Dymphna to forget about writing, for there was a much more urgent issue at hand.

"Flee this fortress, flee the land!
Your father's madness has fully ripened
and just as the rotten fruit falls from the tree, so
his sense topples to the depths,
and all the angels of Heaven
and the demons of Hell
will surely despair
lest you flee,
flee from here!
Flee!
For it is the king's will
to make poor Dymphna his queen!"

The panic-stricken princess looked to Lilith for help.

"If I try to overcome the king here, his demonic fortress walls will crash upon us in wrath!" Lilith exclaimed. "We must do as the spirit says."

So they would flee.

"But whence shall we flee?" asked the girls to the Marquis in unison.

"Out the window, across the sea, to Belgium," replied he. "I will assign you a guardian, and you must make the journey at once!"

Dymphna grabbed some essentials—her kunzite rosary, journal, a couple CDs, her favorite moisturizer and makeup, and some bejeweled ornaments, and threw on a gray velvet travelling cloak. She handed Lilith her mother's knee-length black suede, since the girls were accustomed to lying about in their lingerie, and there was no time now to retrieve Lilith's clothing from where they'd left it beside the Jacuzzi. And out the window, Malte, the attendant with scarlet hair and slippers, and a child's voice like his master's, ushered the girls, blowing a soft zephyr breeze till they reached the ground safely. Lights streaked out from the window as the legion of demons followed the Marquis home, but Malte protected the girls and ran with them through the countryside. They would have to travel day and night to reach the channel safely, but indeed, their speed tripled many times in his custody. The girls scarcely lost their breath before they had reached the shore, which they'd have to cross on the midnight ferry.

Lilith dug around in her purse looking for something, anything, she could offer as toll.

Her agitated fingers rummaged into the corners and folds, the lipsticks and wrappers and bits of glitter getting stuck in her nails. Then her fingers fell upon a small vial she hadn't thought about in years. She pulled it out and hurriedly held it up to the ferryman's lantern to see if anything was left inside.

"Sorry, lady, I only accept the common currency of this kingdom for a toll."

The girls didn't have any actual money, and Dymphna wasn't about to part with her royal accoutrements for a ferry ride. She looked at Lilith, worried.

"This dove's blood is blessed, you idiot," Lilith told the man, who looked poor and wretched, with hollow eyes and demeanor. "Wish upon it, and it becomes your grub for several days, a rendezvous with a fabulous courtesan for a night, or a pure gold coin for an hour! Now off with us!"

The Ferryman didn't question any further. He pushed the ferry out into the channel and they were off.

The girls' flat in Gheel was situated on a thin cobblestone street near downtown. For many months, Lilith and Dymphna lived a secret life, concealing their identities and making their living by giving clairvoyant readings. Having arrived in the city months ago knowing no one, their business now had an extensive waiting list full of illustrious and aristocratic patrons. Their flat was small, of a comfortable size, but by no means humble. Gilt furniture upholstered with white and peach striped silks, and a large domed birdcage housing a pair of canaries, who came and went freely. The flat was complete with a harpsichord and miniature pipe organ that sounded like an orchestra of flutes.

The girls quite forgot about their perilous journey and precarious situation, and simply enjoyed their new life.

Perhaps they had abandoned caution too soon, for one day King Damon stormed into the flat with greasy hair and a face like a burn. His ministers pinned Dymphna down and restrained Lilith, while he forcibly violated his daughter and then cut off her head with his clunky sword. Lilith seized King Damon by the hair and quick as a bat, impaled him with his own sword and knocked in his ministers' skulls with her elbows. Vengeance was swift, but alas, came too late for her dear bosom friend, whose head had flown across the room, landing on the walnut bureau, eyes half open as if gazing quizzically at the whole scene of fresh bloody corpses strewn about the fancy rugs and furniture.

Lilith sealed the princess' body and head in a silver reliquary and immediately prepared a large vat of boiling water into which she threw the bodies of these horrible men. She discarded the flesh and broke all the bones so they would fit snugly into two pillowcases. She then hailed a cab to take her to what would be her friend's final resting place, a hill overlooking the city. The reliquary was interred in a stone tomb-like chapel built from the teeth of murderers as well as generic famished spirits that Lilith released from her jewelry by smashing it all upon the mountain out of grief. This hill now became a holy hill.

Lilith stomped the remaining bones in her pillowcases into a pile of dust, onto which she spit and pissed and bled, then through incantation, conjured into a terrifying monster. She charged the monster with the task of guarding Dymphna's tomb from those unworthy to be in the presence of her relics.

Grief-stricken and despondent, Lilith retreated back to the black castle she had abandoned so many years before. It had fallen into ruin, but the sorceress found comfort in her old four-poster with brocade drapes, which now doubled as a hostel for larvae of various fashions.

After many years, Lilith's mourning ran its course and her mood lifted. The castle once again drew servants, attendants, courtiers and lovers. What creature of this forest could resist the sorceress when she was in a good mood? Soon the master bathroom had to be remodeled with the bath in the very center of the room on a three-tiered pedestal, to accommodate the mass of attendants who showed up to help out at bath time. And each meal featured countless lavish courses, most of which were completely wasted and ended up in the trash. Just like the old days.

The Trespastress

ilith was lounging in her favorite tower overlooking the lake and the pine trees that feast on the doves that fill the sky. She was brushing her hair with a Victorian solid gold hairbrush that had been a gift from the monks of the Abbey of Lucerne. Matteus, her faithful young sweetheart, was keeping the sorceress company and massaging her feet. Lilith took Matteus with her everywhere she went, for he always knew how to entertain her with his wit and charm her with his smile.

"Mathian, darling, can you use some of the pomegranate massage oil on my feet? It always keeps me fresh."

Matteus ran to the bathroom to grab the oil. "Oh Mistress, you rascally old rag you, when will you stop relying on the blood of a nut-seed to stay young?" Matteus liked to tease her about her pomegranate seeds.

"Come along, darling," said Lilith as she welcomed Matteus into her arms for a cuddle. Matteus then promptly began to fuck Lilith with all the magic and freshness of a first kiss. After nearly six hours, they both achieved orgasm at the same time. While she was gyrating with pleasure, Lilith often hurt her darling Matteus, grasping him intensely between her hands. Matteus didn't mind this kind of treatment, for he actually enjoyed that sort of ego-obliterating physical pain that made him feel appreciated by his mistress.

As they were lying on the crumpled bedsheets, the antique phone rang shrilly. Lilith pressed her finger to her lover's lips. "Don't answer it just yet, my love," she whispered.

A moment later, Samantha, the head governess, came rushing into the room to announce the phone call. Damn it. All Lilith wanted was some peace and quiet after a good fuck.

Lilith slowly picked up the phone as she glared at the governess, who apologetically backed out of the room. Coiling her finger into a lovely chestnut lock of Matteus's hair, Lilith contrived a saccharine, lighthearted greeting to the caller.

A creaky old voice spoke into Lilith's ear. Matteus's eyes grew wide with curiosity as he saw the look of astonishment on his mistress's face.

"This is Lady Mille Larmes, your neighbor on the other side of the lake. . ." said the creaky old voice. "I thought you should know that there's been a strange girl trespassing in your garden by moonlight."

"Who is this?" Lilith demanded. The old voice ignored her question and blabbered on.

"Yes, by moonlight each night a trespastress enters your garden and sings to the flowers. Other creatures accompany her from the forest, but wait outside the gate, apparently too timid to follow her in."

Lilith disentangled herself from Matteus's limbs and left him on the bed staring at her with concern, as she carried the phone to the bay window.

The old voice continued. "This trespastress sings bizarre soaring poetic frill to the flowers and they grow and weep a tincture. She proceeds all around your gardens and courtyards while everyone in your castle is asleep. The girl is quite cavalier, and moves about as if your gardens were her own."

"Who is this!" Lilith demanded. She had no

neighbors. Besides, everyone knew that there was never a time when everyone in her castle was asleep, for merriment and intimate affairs carried on all the time, and the castle was known as a bastion of celebration even in the darkest hours.

Once again, the voice ignored Lilith's questions and continued. ". . . as the girl completes her song and trails back into the night, several of the creatures following her, dressed in dark cowls, scurry into your garden and collect the tincture from the flowers in little glass vials. They move nervously and with stealth, and after they have contained that substance, they hurry back into the forest again."

Lilith was annoyed. Was this a joke? The voice was like none she had ever heard. Like a grandmother hanging from a rafter. Who was this caller, bearing this inauspicious report? Was her tale to be trusted? Who could this trespassing songstress be, who would dare insinuate herself into Lilith's garden? There were too many disturbing aspects to this phone call.

"Thank you, and good bye!" Lilith exclaimed, and hung up the phone abruptly.

Lilith sped wildly around the room, shoving pillows, and other objects around, peering under the bed and in the closet, into drawers and behind statuettes.

"What are you looking for?" asked Matteus, who just wanted to relax.

"My crystal scrying ball, damn it!" cried Lilith. "I need to get to the bottom of this!"

"I saw it yesterday by that dish on the window seat, I think," said Matteus, yawning and snuggling his bare body more deeply into the mess of lilac-scented, periwinkle sheets.

Lilith flung the pillows she was holding onto a loveseat, and bolted back over to the window seat. Sure enough, her crystal scrying ball was lying against a silver dish that still bore the remains of yesterday's dinner—some glazed and sugared brussels sprouts and lemon buckwheat cake crumbs scattered about, both on and off the dish.

Lilith snatched up the crystal ball, and pivoted brusquely to kiss Matteus's cheek and rub his naked back. "Thanks, honey," she told him, and ran off to do her scrying work, which she always did alone.

Lilith stormed through the black tourmaline corridors in a histrionic fit, waving her crystal ball around her and blurting outbursts about "that accursed neighbor, that accursed trespass." In theory, she liked to keep the goings-on in her chambers strictly confidential, but would inevitably draw attention to her activities every time with these kind of antics—making a big fuss about her crystal ball, or dramatically running off to her secret chamber only to peep back into the pantry minutes later, to ask the cook for a pinch of nutmeg for her potion.

As Lilith was storming purposefully through a long corridor, she passed the head governess.

"Samantha! Find out who's been stealing into my garden late at night!" While Lilith would, of course, consult her oracle, it couldn't hurt to have Samantha investigate the situation the old fashioned way.

Before Samantha could formulate a question about this strange request, Lilith was rounding the corner at the end of the hall, her peach silk nightgown flowing out behind her.

Samantha was used to Lilith's absurd bouts of rage and paranoia, and the governess always did what she could to humor her mistress. Despite her dramatic and sometimes irritable nature, Lilith was quite benevolent, always indulging her household with luxurious boons. If Samantha ever found herself getting roused or offended, she had only to think of her opulent bedroom, hung with fine silks and carpeted with the skins of mystical beasts that had died of natural causes.

Samantha chose Adelbrand, a daydreamy cook's assistant, for the task of keeping watch in the garden. Adelbrand was given to romantic, fantastical notions, and offered to track and follow any trespassers. To this, Samantha just replied, "Fine, fine," not seriously suspecting anything to come of it.

Adelbrand's New Life

delbrand was doodling in his composition book when the group arrived. He stayed in the shadows for a while, watching, then stashed the comp book into his satchel as they snuck off.

The boy followed the strange, corrupt-looking party into the forest. He took care to stay far enough behind so that he wouldn't be noticed. In the distance, the girl in white was lightly flitting down the path, as if in a trance, and unaware of the robed figures. For a while, they stuck to the path, then started moving through the underbrush and over knotted tree roots. By the time Adelbrand's ankles got excessively tired and he wanted to turn back, he realized that he was completely disoriented. Since humans lost in this particular forest usually ended up devoured by witches or impaled by wild yales, Adelbrand figured he was probably safer following this uncertain group than to try his luck in the forest by himself. He resolved to follow the party to its destination.

They reached a wall. An enormous wall, gray stone, overgrown with vines and tendrils, corners of bricks crumbling and arched windows deep-set in the bricks, beyond which inaccessible halls receded into courtyards where the daylight was beginning to break. Adelbrand was sweaty, totally exhausted and freezing, and he had lost track of the party he was following. He awkwardly shifted between the wall and the overreaching trees. The roots pushed against the base of the wall, and at times he was forced to slither his skinny body narrowly between the wall and a tree. At some point, he reached the end of the wall and found himself alongside another wall. Then maybe there was another wall. In some wall or another were locked doors with heavy iron padlocks and ornate hinges. This was scary. Adelbrand remembered he hadn't finished his homework and started getting annoyed at himself. He always wasted his time doodling in his composition book when he was supposed to be doing homework. But Lilith herself had asked that someone find out what was going on in her garden, and somehow Adelbrand had had the ridiculous idea to follow them. He had just about reached the end of this last wall, and he had an erection and had to pee.

One of the heavy wooden doors creaked open and a boy appeared. Adelbrand knew his erection would be obvious, so he turned to the side and looked at the boy over his shoulder, attempting to make this appear like some sort of natural affect. The boy looked about the same age as Adelbrand himself. Adelbrand was the nerdy type, with glasses, a little tall and skinny, with a couple zits, but very cute. He was shaking a bit out of nervousness and cold, when the boy invited him in. Adelbrand's clothes were all damp and dirty from walking in pursuit all night long, and he felt just horrible.

"I'm Johnny," the boy said. Johnny seemed perfect in every way. Fun, witty, at ease.

A thousand voices in Adelbrand's head were telling him, "DON'T GIVE YOURSELF AWAY YOU'RE A SPY MAKE SOMETHING UP JUST PLAY IT COOL, MAN" but he was so exhausted and nervous that right away he told Johnny everything. He confided his fears about being found out as a spy in this place, and tortured or killed, but Johnny assured him that he would definitely be safe. Adelbrand wasn't convinced.

"We'll say you're the son of my childhood governess, and that you've travelled here all the way from Bavaria to visit me," Johnny suggested, taking Adelbrand by the hand. This kind gesture calmed Adelbrand down, and his heart fluttered a little. Adelbrand agreed to the tale.

"But first," scolded Johnny affectionately, "let's get you into some proper clothes!" Adelbrand self-consciously looked down at his damp, dirty, ripped clothes. Johnny stripped off Adelbrand's shirt and tossed it into the rag bin. Then Johnny fumbled through a luxurious mound of clean laundry, still warm from the dryer, until he found just the right outfit for his new friend. A soft, form-fitting but extremely comfortable, low-neck tabard which showed off Adelbrand's collar bone nicely. After dressing him up, Johnny put his hands on Adelbrand's ribs and gazed at his face encouragingly, as if with pride at a brand new doll. Johnny himself was wearing cut-off light blue jean shorts and a very worn-in off-the-shoulder highland brigandine with magickal logos covering it, that mesmerized the eye. Was this place even real?

That afternoon, Johnny proudly paraded his new friend through the mansion. Adelbrand was still nervous he'd be found out, but it was the kind of place where people were always arriving and departing, so his presence was accepted without any suspicion.

Adelbrand packed so much fun into that afternoon. First Johnny introduced him to Hildegard. They didn't exchange a single word but stared into each others' eyes for a long time, and then she kissed him on the hand and put daffodils all over his hair. Adelbrand blushed and, not wanting to accept this gracious gesture without offering something in return, reached into the pocket of his tabard and pulled out an old black, white, gold and purple bar mitzvah invitation from someone nobody knew, and gave it to her. Then all three of them went swimming in the pool with a couple hilarious girls named Sasha and Penelope, who were non-stop talking manically about being chased by the police and haughty girls at the mall, and asking Adelbrand personal questions about his life and passions.

Afterward, Adelbrand played frisbee out on the field with Johnny, Josh and Arcady. Adelbrand thought Josh and Arcady were really cool, and he felt a bit awkward and intimidated at first—but the elf princes laughed infectiously at everything he said, as if he'd just made their day. Then, at the devil's hour, many gathered in the bath house to relax in deep marble basins of steaming drugged brine. Following that, there was an assortment of ornaments and garments. There were fresh spirulina truffles spiced with ginger and cloves on a tray, and a grand alcove by a bay window with several urns of holy body parts steeped in fine medicinal oils, with which all the dwellers were generously massaging one another. Adelbrand was still a bit self-conscious, trying to say the right thing and hold himself in the right posture, which of course made everything he said and did appear endearingly awkward. But once Arcady offered him a shot of holy basil tinctured rum, Adelbrand started loosening up and kicked off his shoes and his cares a bit.

Adelbrand spent most of the summer at the castle. He went back home now and then, mostly for his crumhorn lessons, and with increasing reluctance. One day, out by the lake, he started complaining about having to go back.

"It's just so much better here at Rupertsberg!" Adelbrand whined.

"Well," said Josh, his face looking as marvelous and flawlessly bright as ever, and his white hair dazzling in the sunlight, "why don't you just stay here?" Josh was always very down-to-earth and practical.

"But I have to go back to school," Adelbrand said dejectedly. "Junior year. Yeck."

"Just transfer to Forest Whispers," said Hildegard. "It's only a couple miles from here, and you could bike to school."

Adelbrand didn't find this idea plausible at all. "I can't," he grumbled, crossing his arms in annoyance. "It just won't work."

Hildegard gave up and had a glass of elecampane wine.

Josh kept questioning Adelbrand about possibly transferring to Forest Whispers, and although the poor kid couldn't give an adequate reason why not, he seemed totally stuck on it not working out. Adelbrand had a tendency to be stubborn and self-sabotaging. He gave a bunch of ridiculous excuses, from needing to "finish what he started at Thornspencer Academy" (whatever that meant), to being absolutely sure that his parents wouldn't let him (Hildegard told him to just ask them and see, but Adelbrand was not hearing it), to really wanting to go on the Junior camping trip at Thornspencer. This last one was particularly ridiculous, since Adelbrand had declined to go on a camping trip with Josh and some other guys the week before, due to his hatred of camping. Not to mention the fact that Adelbrand had complained several times about how he couldn't really relate to anyone back at Thornspencer, and no one really "got" him. Sure, he had some friends—Brad and Agatha, for example—who were fine to hang out with, but they were always talking about boring stuff like their exercise routines or politics. Their company was ok, but Adelbrand never really felt like he could be himself around them. Finally, he had found a group of friends that he really "connected with" (Adelbrand's own words), and yet, he seemed intent on putting up roadblocks to the idea of moving into the castle with them. Josh didn't get it.

Finally, Adelbrand gave Josh an angry, hurt look, and blurted out, "You just don't get it, Josh. You're an elf prince, you had everything handed to you on a silver platter your whole life, and you just can't understand that life could be anything but easy, free, and wonderful for anyone!" Then he burst into tears and dramatically ran away.

This was completely ridiculous, and Adelbrand had to have known it. Sure, Josh had grown up as an elf prince, always got everything he wanted as a child, was beautiful and loved by everyone, and got to ride everywhere in a horse-drawn carriage and eat whatever he wanted at any time. But Josh had also spent several years as a prisoner in an atrocious dungeon full of rotten garbage and decaying victims, lonely and tortured by a demon every day for several years, and when he started high school he was meek and had few friends. Adelbrand had heard Josh talk about these difficult years of torture and loneliness, but apparently had a selective memory when it interfered with his own agenda of remaining trapped in victim mode.

A few days later, when Adelbrand went back home, he did end up asking his parents if he could go live in the castle with his friends, and transfer to Forest Whispers. At first they wouldn't hear of it, but when he wouldn't drop it over several days, they finally gave in—under the condition that he still come back every week for his crumhorn lesson and dinner. They agreed to sign his guardianship over to Josh, so he could go register at the new school.

Lilith, on the other hand, was highly suspicious about Adelbrand's new friends. But she'd pretty much lost interest in pursuing them, since she was so busy with her new rare gourmet bratwursts-from-around-the-world business.

"I promise you, Ma'am, they're great kids," Adelbrand told her.

"Maybe one of these days I'll invite them over for a feast," said Lilith.

Part III

The Sorceress's Feast

ne day, I suppose it was around prom season, a large marble slab arrived in the mail. On it was engraved, in comic sans font, an invitation to join Lilith for a feast at her palace the following evening. We were all very excited about this event, and Hildegard made me promise to go.

"The devil's hour calls for a change of garb," chirped Arcady, as he shut himself in his room again, leaving Josh and me in the hall with awkward, sullen afternoon sunshine slanting into the dust. I yawned and swayed a bit, since I tend towards fatigue, confusion and dizziness at this time of day.

"He's quite right," said Josh, patting me on the head. I crumbled into Josh's arms and let him half-carry me into my room and lay me on the bed where I waited for him to find me something more suitable to wear. How suddenly anxiety and confusion strike. I feel at times so perplexed at my existence that I can't move. How nice it is to have handsome loving guardians like my two elf princes to take care of me. I can't even recall how I ever managed to live without them. Even now, they seem to just barely keep my fragile heart held together by a string.

Josh brought me a nice linen doublet, black jeans, and my royal blue maneki-neko cloak (with little emblems of the lucky cat all over it in different colors). I hadn't worn that cloak for weeks and had all but forgotten about it. He helped me button the doublet up all the way, then frowned and ripped it open to the waist, sending all the little pearl buttons skittering across the parquet. Definitely a sexier look. Then he spritzed me with some refreshing holy water that Hildegard and some of the nuns had made with essence of cat's eye and oleander. I felt completely renewed and ready for our outing.

Arcady met us back in the hall. He had changed into maroon lacquer greaves and matching plackart over a short cream tunic, leaving his thighs completely bare. The look was completed with a turquoise cape and the brass crown that Hildegard had criticized earlier. Only Arcady could pull off garnets, pearls, brass and turquoise all together like that.

Josh wasn't obsessed with fashion like Arcady, and just wore a mid-length tunic covered with tiny bits of mother of pearl which gave it a glorious sheen—almost as if the tunic were vying to compete with the natural luster of Josh's own skin tone, and failing tragically.

Hildegard wore an absolutely sheer ankle-length chasuble gathered at the arms, over a black brocade bodice cut just under the breasts, tight black leather pants, and black patent leather stiletto boots, her hair in many cornrows, and her lips the color of autumn rain.

Adelbrand had left much earlier to help out at Lilith's, and I have no idea what he was wearing.

We all went out into the open air.

The cawing of the birds and the whining of the bears. A loud swan yawned.

We walked all the way around the lake, down and up a hill, and saw her black tourmaline spires just ahead. Like midnight freeways running up into the sky, with little lights twinkling.

The sorceress's palace was no disappointment.

The driveway was paved with white-veined black marble, all perfectly glossy and polished, as if wet. We were met at the door by a young boy who stared and bowed, then led us through austere, vast, polished black rooms linked together uniformly through high cathedral arches. In one enclosed section of the castle, Josh caught my attention and pointed at the ceiling, about one sky's height above, where a spiral staircase led into the darkness of a belltower. I got scared. Other guests, every one of them immaculately dressed and with ambiguous facial expressions, began to accumulate around us.

In the process of going from one hall to another, and into the large heavily black-mirrored dining room, I lost Josh and Hildegard as a stream of guests cut through us. With masses of unfamiliar beings overtaking the area around the table, I clung to Arcady so I wouldn't have to sit between two people I didn't know. I didn't feel like dealing with strangers. *Oh why did I come here at all?*, I fretted. But Hildegard would have killed me if I'd stayed home. I tried to scowl at her from across wherever she was, but when I finally spotted her among the unknown beings, she was offering her hand to an androgenous polite bowing head for a kiss.

Lilith seemed very warm and kind, smiling radiantly in rose silk, with a gold ouroboros girdle that looped around and tastefully framed her breasts, which were left bare. She wore her hair piled high up in coils that pleased the eye and dripped with bloodred encrustments. Matteus, her close companion, sat at her side and kept flicking her teardrop earring with his fingernail when he wanted attention. Each time he did this, a pat on the head and a ruffle of his hair seemed to satisfy him for about five seconds.

Arcady told me to count the number of courses served so I'd have something to do with my anxiety. Every time a new course was ready, a boy with perfect chin-length yellow hair resembling a sheet, and a circlet atop his head, marked with the head of a bear about to strike, would appear in the arched doorway and clap his hands twice rapidly, signaling an army of diligent waitstaff to snatch up our dishes, polish the table clean, and place the new course in front of us on gigantic plates. The courses came and went so swiftly, it wasn't possible to finish a single one. There was tender yam daisy, black hellebore honey bisque, roast peacock served with feathers intact and the beak and feet gilded, bloodwort stew served on slabs of whale fat, chestnut dandelion knödel with a lavender sauce... it seemed like Lilith never got tired of laughing and eating. I won't bore the dear reader with an exhaustive description, for in any case I lost track around course thirteen, when the guy on my left started talking to me.

His name was Abriel, and he was from Brittany and wore a black sash. Once we started talking, I was sorry I hadn't struck up a conversation sooner. He was a fascinating kind of guy. He told me he'd been here at Lilith's place for several years. He'd been a travelling salesman and was going door to door with some girl scouts he'd kidnapped and was trying to raise. They'd all showed up at Lilith's door selling Girl Scout cookies. She didn't want anything, in fact the idea of it offended her. Thin mints are disgusting, basically just crumbs stuck together with chemicals and goo.

Lilith had then invited Abriel and the girls inside and held them prisoner, until they all became like family to her. Since then, they'd never left. Abriel pointed out three teen girls, Odette, Solange, and Beatrice Rose, at various points around the enormous table. These were three of his troupe. The girls seemed pretty and well-behaved.

Odette was laughing demurely while talking

to the boy next to her; Solange was chewing thoughtfully; and Beatrice Rose seemed charmingly engaged in conversation with Adelbrand, who was sitting next to her.

Abriel and I talked some more, about feasts and the weather and the arts, boring small-talk stuff. Did you know that all the wonderful, rich earth tones in the icons of the Byzantine churches had been painted with the blood of slain heretics? Then he asked me questions about my life, interests, and views on current events.

Suddenly a shriek rang out. Beatrice Rose's red face pointed across the table, in Lilith's direction.

"Ma'am!" Beatrice Rose shouted. Lilith put her fork down. Beatrice Rose had corn kernels all over her bare hands. "I can't believe you had this served with butter! You know I can't eat this, Ma'am!" She looked like she was about to cry or attack.

Lilith suddenly looked exhausted. She clanged her little bell and the pageboy appeared.

"Len, please rinse the butter off this for Beatrice Rose," she said as she reached across the table, picked up Beatrice Rose's plate, and handed it to the pageboy. Her voice sounded strained. "I'm so sorry, dear," Lilith told the girl. The pageboy ran off with Beatrice Rose's dish.

Beatrice Rose quivered with rage. "And you know that ever since I was a girl I've had such fond memories of eating corn on the cob on those little silver prongs, I don't understand why you would have the corn so mercilessly cut from its cob, it takes so much more effort to eat!" She started to sob into her dinner napkin.

"I'm so sorry, honey," Lilith said. "I had no idea you wanted it on the cob, I was so foolish to be thinking only of our guests." Lilith actually did sound sorry. The pageboy scampered in and set the unbuttered corn in front of the brat.

Beatrice Rose shoveled the corn into her mouth with more sobs. She screamed, "But I like it on the cob because of the way it massages my teeth!"

Lilith turned to the pageboy, who was still standing there attentively, and told him to see if he could fetch some cobs out of the compost. "Really, dear," she said to Beatrice Rose, "I had no idea this meant so much to you."

The pageboy ran out again and came back with a ragged cob on a silver dish, which he set in front of Beatrice Rose. She started chewing on the edge of it, and this seemed to calm her down. I resumed my conversation with Abriel as if nothing had happened.

A couple minutes later, we were distracted by another outburst from Beatrice Rose. It seemed she was scolding Adelbrand for eating too fast, and trying to prevent him from eating certain things on his plate. He had resisted her will to control him, and it had escalated until the girl was shouting again. The members of Lilith's household seemed accustomed to ignoring Beatrice Rose's outbursts.

Meanwhile, Josh and Arcady were having a hushed conversation and giggling, and Abriel had struck up a conversation with the lady next to him. Beatrice Rose got up from her seat and stormed out of the room. I was feeling overwhelmed by all the noise and everything, and felt the urge to go outside. Just then, I saw Hildegard standing by Lilith and whispering something in her ear.

Lilith looked right at me. I hadn't even been introduced to her yet, so I just sat there shocked and nervous, with my mouth open.

"Johann, could you go after her?" Lilith asked, as if we'd known each other forever. "Just try to calm her down a bit, she really responds well to handsome young men such as yourself. Hildegard tells me you're really great at handling these kinds of things." She smiled. "Just bring her back to dinner after she's had a chance to cool off, please."

I obviously couldn't say no, but I was annoyed at Hildegard for volunteering me for this uncomfortable task. I tried to smile politely, and went after Beatrice Rose.

When I caught up with the brat, Beatrice Rose insisted on walking ahead of me. I just followed her. The black marble corridors echoed with our footsteps. A small man was sitting against the wall playing some very sophisticated tune on his lute. I tossed $2 in the little dish in front of him.

"How much did you give him?" Beatrice Rose suddenly asked. Her face was a jagged triangle of contempt.

"$2," I said.

"I can't believe you would give him your money," she said angrily.

"Well, I liked his playing, and I wanted to pay him, so what."

"Well, where do you get your money? It's not even yours. You're spoiled."

"I don't know," I snapped back at her, "I guess I get my money from the Vatican, it just arrives every month. I have no idea from where. I'm not going to argue with you that I'm not spoiled, but you're being very unpleasant."

"I'm leaving, I don't need to put up with this abuse," Beatrice Rose declared.

"Look, just calm down and let's get back to dinner. I don't want to miss dessert."

Beatrice Rose pointed her chin in the opposite direction and ran off. I tried to catch up with her, but lost the bitch.

In some dark series of black marble rooms whose ceilings echoed with the silent laughter of human skulls carved out of semiprecious stones, I got lost. I tripped over some legs.

It was a lady sitting on a couch. She had an old face and a short dress with stockings. She had me sit down next to the slit in her dress, from which a leg peeked out. On the other side of me, a lapis lazuli skull grinned from the hearthstone. I am told that when stone is carved into the shape of a human skull, it develops human brain-like characteristics and the instinct to communicate.

"Would you like to see the treasures of this house?" asked the lady, who was sitting uncomfortably close.

"What?" I thought about Beatrice Rose and felt nervous about failing to do what Lilith asked of me.

"Lilith collects unscathed children from all

around the world, and keeps them prisoners here," the lady clarified. "Do you want to see them?"

"I guess so," I said.

Lady Freymiller's Dungeon

ady Freymiller had ways of arriving and departing through caverns and secret winding passages. At one point we had to step over an underground stream full of snapping eels, which nearly caught me by the ankle. I probably should have just stayed at the dinner table.

Finally we reached a locked gate of floor-to-ceiling golden bars. She took a key from her purse and unlocked it so I could go in and play with the prisoners, who were all naked and leapt around like dancing leopards.

"Sshhhh," she said as she closed the gate behind me, "they don't actually know they are prisoners. Don't tell them. This is their world."

The first guy who danced up to me was Limlal. He was black as obsidian, bald and gorgeous. He took me downstairs.

The stairs went spiraling around and around. A chariot, drawn by doves, was waiting for us outside the window.

"Um, where are we going?" I asked Limlal, as he took my hand and led me into the chariot.

"I want to show you my world," he said. What is a world? World = prison?

From the sky, the countryside looked completely different. The air was a complete chill, but Limlal seemed comfortable despite being naked. The chariot gained speed.

"Wait, where are we going?" I asked again. Limlal's face was so beautiful that no amount of staring at it would ever satisfy me. I found it impossible to think of anything else, so I had no ability to pay attention to his words.

"I want to show you my home," Limlal told me.

I saw angels tearing through the sky in every direction, passing by our chariot. I let the naked boy hold me with my head against his stomach and his arms all around me because I was cold. I changed into the dark garment that he gave me.

An iron column, fearful to behold. The height

of the column occupied the whole of the sky. I still couldn't understand how Limlal managed to go out in this bitter cold without wearing any clothes. No person who is still in the rottenness of flesh is able to understand, he told me.

The column had three sides, and its edges were as sharp as swords. The chariot landed near the open door. Limlal took my hand. The air still froze. "This is one of the four watchtowers of the universe. We are going to leave the bounds of the world," Limlal said.

"What is a world?" I asked.

"Like an apple full of maggots, a world is a mass or globule of matter infected by parasitic influences."

A woman clothed in the golden ray of light held by a dove hovering in the air greeted us on the pavement in front of the watchtower. She endowed me with a magic mantle to keep me warm on the journey, for without such protection, an ordinary person would surely die. I know it's superficial, but what I really liked about the mantle was its dark purple, almost black color, and how elegantly it flowed around me everywhere.

People were running around the tower, using whips on each other. This was a time of war.

Limlal told me that only if I took off my clothes could I become invincible like him. But it was still too cold.

We came up to a crowd, in front of which a wonderfully large worm was lying on its back. Limlal hissed loudly and the crowd dispersed. He slapped the worm on the belly and it flipped around. We mounted the worm and galloped away, across the drab countryside, Limlal in front and I behind with my hands on his warm bare thighs.

"Where are we going?" I asked again, already forgetting. Limlal dug his heels into the worm's sides and we galloped faster.

"We're going to a land of freedom. My home, the City of the Pyramids."

"How far is it?" I asked.

"We should be there in three days."

I lay my cheek against the back of Limlal's shoulder and fell asleep.

In my dream, a jaguar came to find me. I was a marble couple sleeping in one another's arms underground. The jaguar was Hildegard, and came with the sound of a bell that signifies the turning of a page in a children's storybook.

I woke up aching all over, crooked and numb from the cold journey. We were still galloping on that worm, across a desolate countryside.

The next night I dreamed I was a water spirit and Hildegard was a zigzag. I was concealed in a perfect sapphire the size of an ostrich egg, smuggled into the hinterlands disguised as a blue sorbet. Limlal was biking me across a border. I can't wait for this sorbet to melt, I am so much closer to experiencing love for the first time.

I woke up with my face wet with drool against Limlal's back. Still galloping over hills and across the desert, the sun was breaking. The days I spent in a trance, as we continued to gallop endlessly over sunken terrain that resembled the trenches left when large cities or teeth are evacuated and destroyed.

Night came again, finally. This time I dreamed I was a pimento on the point of an obelisk. Hildegard was a tornado that carried me in her loving arms to a distant mountain peak and left me there. I implanted in the soil, then grew to be a powerful but inert king. The sunrise wouldn't stop happening.

Hildegard, a sword made of space-grade amethyst, separated my limbs and head from my body. I had to be separated, then boiled up until I was completely cooked, then my limbs reunited over and over again. This was merely preparation for the next stage of separation.

In order now to transition from being a whole, complete person, to a collection of separate parts, I had to successfully cross over the sea of snapping jaws. My throat burned as I approached, even as I began to think of such a place. The harsh teeth clanged with hunger like scissor blades striking each other as if trying blindly to fuck. Each soulless lover of this sea fucks mindlessly while gazing at his own reflection in the bedside vanity mirror as all slowly age and decompose into gnarled bones rubbing and crumbling through the sea of steaming flesh.

I was told, by the cute boy sitting at the desk and guarding the gate to the sea of snapping jaws, that the City of the Pyramids lay just beyond. Why, even here in the desert, seconds away from the destruction of my precious human body, will this cute boy refuse to look at me with interest? I dropped four of my ribs into the toll bin, and a huge black greasy-haired rat with missing eyeballs shot out from underneath the boy's chair and gobbled up my offering, faster and more aggressively than a piece of burned toast leaping from a toaster.

I enter the sea and everything transforms into bliss. Finally I can become unburdened by meaning. Everything I've ever wanted or needed now has the chance to die.

I have no longer any parts.

Hildegard appeared out of the empty sky dressed in gold culottes and a raspberry Marchesa shawl, holding a vial. She annointed the portion of space that signified my self.

"Don't worry, baby, all that exists is imagination," she said as her fingers traced through the air, my entrails and heart, had I a body. "Nothing can be created or destroyed, only imagined. How do you want to be created, so that you can be a match for your enemies?"

"Who are my enemies?"

"Your enemy is the world of form and death," she told me. "You know, Johnny, I might not always be around to protect you."

"Then please don't create me in human form," I replied. "Give me the head of an owl with the teeth of a tiger, the neck of a cobra, the claws of an ocelot, the tail of a rooster, the wings of a bat and the dick of a dolphin."

Hildegard cast a circle in the chaos, then sprinkled some of the tincture into the air with whispered prayer. I appeared as that majestic beast, licked Hildegard's cheek with my owl's tongue, and took flight into the City of the Pyramids.

I woke up feeling dehydrated, my cheek plastered to Limlal's bare back and all my muscles sore and aching. It was pale blue-white daylight. Limlal helped me disembark the worm, who flowed away across the land. I could hardly see anything through this bleary storm. I wiped the sleep from my eyes.

Limlal had to leave me because he said I wasn't quite ready to enter the City. A piece of impure substance has to be dissolved and reconstituted many times to remove the impurities completely.

He pointed in some direction. "I will meet you there," he said, and disappeared.

I walked across the flooded landscape trenching through the mud in the direction Limlal suggested, although all directions were meaningless. My face turned into a peacock face, then back into a human face with bright moving parts. I became two people. We hated to look at each other because I couldn't deal with the fact that I had no true self. I had fallen under a blind power.

It took us ninety days to reach the gate to the City. We sat facing each other. *I'm not going to have sex with this copy of myself.* We refused to have sex with each other. I stared into his eyes, which were yellow rectangles.

After ten days and ten hours of resisting, we finally gave up. Fucking him is not unlike the co-mingling of sin and virtue. I can't get his thigh out of my mind.

I've learned how to fuck myself longer than day and night. The angel of our fucking leaned down to remind me that there is an end to life and death.

"Thanks, babe," I slapped the angel's buttock.

Somewhere there is an end to Life and Death. Somewhere in God's house is a tomb for the relics of all phenomena. This is called the City of the Pyramids. Some beings call it Heaven.

The City of the Pyramids

he sky of this city is composed of a storm of flaming arrows flying about in all directions. The clouds are made of fire, the trees are made of blood, the people are made of light, and volcanoes spew lava with such force it never falls back to the earth. Skyscrapers crash around everywhere and human beings in the colors of all jewels roam freely through the air.

Limlal took me to his friend's house, a magnificent fortress guarded by rows of black gargoyles striking from the roof and steeples. The towers blazed with living stones who flew like clouds into the sky.

As we walked down the long corridors of black marble streaked with white veins, as if a map of the City of Pyramids desires sex, Limlal gently held the back of my neck. Pulsating limbs began disappearing behind open doors everywhere. These bodies seemed naked and crazed. I could scarcely make out any details apart from the ears and skin, which were nice.

We hung out a while in Limlal's bandmate Porter's room, overlooking a huge gushing abyss into the sea. Porter strummed on his banjo while Fear of God, the lead singer, sang about preparing blissful daughters to gaze upon the living God without dying. A couple jumped out the window into the gushing abyss.

I was still clutching the magic mantle tightly around me, because this house, like all of this city, like all of these terrains, like all of these unexplored rooms in Lilith's castle, was cold as naked bones.

Next entered a garlanded boy of a type of delicacy encountered only in undiscovered locales. I wrapped him up with me in my magic mantle, but no matter how hard we fucked, we could not actually unite, for our bodies were in the way. I also noticed that my self, which existed as a highly irritating, tragic factor, did not know how to love this creature. Try as I might, I couldn't get this gorgeous angel, who was murdering my body with inhuman longing, to really see me, for despite the body apparently existing, there is no self, and he gazed through my eyes into the void. Finally I gave up, tossed my clothes and mantle aside, and followed him out the window, toppling into the sea. I have come to the conclusion that reality, whatever one chooses to call it, and whether one understands it to be real or not, cannot be escaped.

I noticed a boy industriously scrubbing the walls and floor each day, paying no attention to anyone. On the third day, he finally turned to face me. It was Danny Barnaby.

"What are you doing here, Danny?! I thought you were dead!" I screamed, and grasped him in total shock and joy. Danny told me how he came to be here, in the City of the Pyramids.

The Precious
Counselor

"When I escaped Disibodenberg, I fled and lived in an outlying slum of Kreuznach. On my sixteenth birthday, I received a most curious, wonderful gift from my neighbor, Adriano. He gave me guardianship of a wise, wish-granting counselor. The counselor was only 36" tall and immeasurably handsome, with glowing features, blonde hair rolling across his forehead as if without a care in the world, and a sparkly gold tan to his flesh. He always wore perfectly-tailored gray velvet trousers and jacket, with a living violet, which never withered, flourishing on the lapel. He spent most of the day in meditation on my mantelpiece, but when I returned home from my long, bitter days as a slave in the factory, he would spring up to greet me and give me all sorts of wise bits of advice and predictions, and occasionally grant me wishes. All he required for sustenance were four peas per day—simple, ordinary peas, the kind that grow everywhere in the countryside, even out of cracks in the sidewalk. By the power of his perfectly accomplished meditation, my counselor was able to subsist endlessly on this grub, only growing lovelier and wiser with each passing year, and never aging a day. He required feeding at the moments the sun made pivotal transformations in the sky, one pea each at sunrise, noon, sunset and midnight. Such was my devotion to my precious counselor that no matter the circumstances, I happily forced myself to his service, returning home from the factory at dawn and noon, and tearing myself out of bed at midnight each day to feed him.

"My love for my counselor grew deeper and deeper each day, as did his own beauty and vitality. Sometimes the inner parts of his eyes looked like green insects' eyes, and from these came the boundless love that can usually only be found in completely dark places with nothing to cling to.

"He started answering my prayers. I discovered treasures, a little at a time, until I was able to pay off my master at the factory, and escape with enough left over to live a life of endless luxury.

"I bought a magnificent cruise ship with spires and towers, tethered it to the cliff just past Jade Bay, and hired the king's personal architect and interior designer to completely gut it and convert it into a mansion. Only the four grand ballrooms remained as they had been, with their dashing chandeliers and scary endless views of water and skies. I even had a special chapel built for my precious counselor, with a throne for him to sit upon all day, a pearl and marble hallway leading nowhere, and pages to bring him flowers at all the hours. But for myself alone I reserved the task of serving him his four peas; and always on a platter of solid gold, despite his dear, modest protests that no such embarrassingly large and expensive platter was called for to serve such a simple fellow as himself.

"Slowly my empire-like home grew strong and populated. I grew accustomed to taking off daily for extravagant errands. Of course, nothing could keep me away from my counselor longer than six hours, so I would always be there to fawn on him and feed him his peas. But I spent the rest of my time on expeditions with numerous friends and acquaintances, who had somehow arrived at my house and taken up residence in its generous apartments. Always, it seemed, some handsome, half-familiar, vague acquaintance arrived at my door in the middle of the afternoon to see if I wanted to accompany him to one of the islands in the bay, or to go collect hallucinogenic barks in the countryside of the mainland, and we'd happily throw away the afternoon laughing and playing and having hilarious perceptions, such as of our eyeballs, having become marble orbs full of gunpowder, ejecting from our heads and crashing all around the courtyards causing much havoc and spectacle.

"As the days and weeks got on, more and more impressive, unrecognizable persons presenting themselves as my dear friends and lovers came for me at all hours of day and night. My life became very difficult to account for, as the days sped by like insatiable burning suns, and I was always either dead asleep, drunk or drugged, or having an intimate conversation with someone I didn't know, or off on some adventure with dear companions who laughed ceaselessly at my jokes, and in fact at every word I spoke, as if anything I could possibly say were the most brilliant thing in the world.

"This completely irresponsible lifestyle continued to the point that one perfect, most amazing day in the summertime, practically raining pollen from the soft blue sky, I was off on several picnics in a wild park on a nearby island, with some boys and girls who were exchanging witty, sarcastic commentary and wearing haplessly thrown-on brocade as well as magnificent jeweled earrings and gossamer capes, and I was listening to their entertaining banter and noticing how perfectly it blended with the gentle laughter-like roar of the brook near our picnic blanket, as the water ran over the smooth pebbles that my friends were sucking on. And suddenly I realized with horror that the sun was well passed the midpoint of the sky, and I had forgotten to feed my precious counselor. I abruptly ended our outing and insisted that we return home immediately. My friends pouted all the way back, and a skinny boy with black hair in his face kept whining very self-indulgently. When we got back to the ship, they kissed me goodbye in a most careless and floppy way, then quickly disappeared into the mansion.

"Utterly alone, I ran to the little chapel, only to find my beautiful, most precious counselor dead. He was sitting in his meditation posture on the mantle as always, but his head was drooping forward, and his skin had already began to shrivel. I had killed the most beautiful person in the world, the one who knew all, and had given to me more generously than a pelican who feeds its young with the blood from its breast.

"So forlorn that life, whether as a slave or as a hapless prince, had lost anything resembling value, I left my mansion without saying goodbye to anyone. I left all those parasitic friends and lovers who were strangers to me. I roamed the country without eating or drinking for days, with the cruel sun beating down upon me. Each moment of internal pain was the most pathetic, insufficient form of retribution for the horror I had committed. I knew I would never be free, never repay this sin. I determined that I would walk constantly, without eating or drinking or sleeping, until I dropped dead. Even that would be insufficient punishment, but it was all that I could offer, for I had no implements with which to mutilate my body. I walked for seven great æons across the barren wasteland, the days were hotter than hell, and the nights were colder and more bitter than the insides of a hag's intestine.

"Finally, I collapsed at the door of this palace. When I woke up, I couldn't imagine how I had ended up in such a magnificent place, with such undeservedly kind company, except no doubt for the kindness of my wise, beloved counselor, generous as he proved to be even beyond the grave. This was the most beautiful house I had ever seen; the tacky ballrooms of my mansion paled in comparison to this palace's yawning chasms of jewels and jagged windows into abysmal oceans.

"I vowed that in order to repay my debt, I would ceaselessly work in this house, cleaning and scrubbing the floors and walls, without sleep, until such a time as I am able to discover where God dwells, find him and murder him."

Danny paused a moment. Then he looked at me warmly. "It's so good to see you, Johnny!" he exclaimed, giving me another embrace. Then straightaway he scampered off, and I wondered if I would ever see him again.

My Loves, My Deaths

spent more days than I can possibly count at that estate, and had many friends, beings and lovers. There was Helga, a bright pirate from a yellow star, Mordred, a pale poet, slender as a pine needle, who loathed sunlight, Ted, a hysterically laughing little pup of a boy with bright black sparrow wings, and Ajax, an angel from the North, who was never without his scarlet chlamys made of snakes. Mordred made me beat him 'til he wept the most beautiful songs, which produced showers of diamonds, and Ajax would rock me to sleep each night until I experienced death in his arms. Then I would wake from a dream of running blissfully through fire.

Each day was nothing but endless band practice, feasting, sex which seemed to occur even without the participation of the body, and ocean dives, tides tossing us around like rags. I wore nothing but the limbs of my companions, and after several nights of dreaming and dying as I have described, I attained an incorruptible body of lightning.

Feasting was endless, heaps of food and other objects piled on altars and floors. A walnut, a diamond, a page or two of indecipherable scripture, a small piece of ruby-red meat, an ocean of clouds, a piece of string knotted by a martyr in throes of death, and many other items both ordinary and extraordinary, and even those which are impossible to perceive, were laid out by the millions on plates that filled the hall. Actual nourishment was highly symbolic, for that body could subsist on imaginary meaningless concepts. We frequently cannibalized each other, and sex that destroyed bodies was also quite common, for bones, blood and flesh were mere ornaments to the blisses we knew. When we grew weary of feasting, all the remains would go out the window, including plates, goblets and silverware, as well as bodies both living and dead, to crash and shatter on the rock and fall into abysses. And next thing you knew, Danny would be scrubbing away from wall to wall, cleaning up the mess.

At last, Limlal told me that it was time to return home. A flock of armless young men with dove wings pulled our chariot by ropes secured in their jaws, my naked thighs clinging to my guardian's hips. My beloved companions waved banners and their wonderful bodies out the windows and flew back and forth and around our heads kissing us goodbye. What a sad farewell to all the flying companions who fell away one by one back to the City of the Pyramids, the palace which got tinier in the distance, the whole city which was now no more than a speck of black glitter in a world.

We rode through the swirling universes again, this time without dreams. I slept completely still against Limlal's body.

I woke toppling back into the tower window, and Limlal walked me down the stairs. He kissed me and promised we would meet again one day. I closed the cage door behind me until I heard a click.

I thanked Lady Freymiller politely, and asked if she could help me find Beatrice Rose. She led me to the girl's bedroom, where Beatrice Rose was lying on her bed, reading a girl's magazine with lots of good tips and pictures of eyes. She seemed relaxed.

"Um, are you ready to go back to dinner?" I asked, bracing myself for an obnoxious response.

"Sure," said Beatrice Rose with an easy-going shrug, as if nothing uncomfortable had happened. She got up and tossed the magazine on her bed and yawned, then smiled at me. I followed her back to the dinner table.

Arcady said they'd just finished a pretty decent chiseled beets galantine served in baskets woven out of asparagus racemosus. And rumor going 'round the table was that dessert was next.

An entire glazed and shining alligator was served on a huge alabaster slab, accompanied by three maidens. They carved it up right in front of us, revealing alternating layers of alligator meat and sponge cake soaked in vervain liqueur. A claw was placed before me on a plate.

By the time we got home, I was so tired I couldn't even make it to bed. I fell asleep in my shoes and everything.

Part IV

Lucifer

od was sitting in session with Sapientia, his therapist. Sapientia was old and withered and white, and wore a stiff purple velvet dress with long sleeves and gold embroidery, and a collar that covered her throat. Her body smelled like a mortuary cellar. Sapientia's business card read

Sapientia
Shamanic Therapist
to the Stars

As Sapientia analyzed Him with a voice that sounded like two sheets of paper being rubbed together absentmindedly, God asked himself why she called herself a "shamanic therapist" and why the hell he paid her $900 an hour when he always left his therapy sessions feeling worse than before. Nevertheless, God decided to pay attention to what she was saying, just in case it bore any validity at all, and since he was paying for it anyway.

"Your problem," Sapientia said with a completely affectless face and a voice that sounded like a fingernail scraping a potato chip, "is that your mother didn't have an orgasm when she conceived you. I know I shouldn't be telling you this, because it could be considered a violation of patient confidentiality," she went on (God's mom had been a long time client and dear friend of Sapientia's, and had confided this to her in one of her own therapy sessions), "but I think it will help you understand your pathology." Her voice resembled an iron nail miserably failing to pleasure itself against a chalkboard.

God stared incredulously at Sapientia's puppet-like, crumpled form propped up against her chair, and thought about killing himself in a million ways.

"Normally," Sapientia continued, "conception is impossible unless the woman has an orgasm. Somehow you squeezed through," she chuckled pleasantly, "but that's why your life, and therefore all of existence, is so fucked up." Sapientia yawned.

A long silence followed, God fidgeted, and Sapientia stared blankly.

Suddenly she crossed her legs and adjusted herself in her chair. "So anyway," Sapientia said intimately, "I've been having funny dreams. Last night I dreamed I was with the girls, and we couldn't find our beach ball. It was so funny."

As usual, God left Sapientia's manor feeling dejected, powerless and irritated. He felt like they never got anywhere in their sessions. One of these days, God thought to himself, he'd fire Sapientia and find someone else to talk to.

God decided to buy a tape. He stopped by Amoeba Records and bought an old single of one of his favorite bands, Butter Tortilla, which he had listened to all the time in middle school. He hadn't heard Butter Tortilla in ages, so he greedily rushed back to his car and immediately stuffed the tape into his car stereo. God played the song over and over on auto-reverse and cried his whole way home through traffic, the sunset blaring in his eyes, with people, life, merriment of which he was not a part, going on in the dirty streets around him.

God stopped briefly at Whole Foods on his way home, where he ate several samples of key lime cheesecake, stuck his grubby hands into the bulk bins and stole some chocolate-covered almonds and roasted macadamia nuts which he stuffed into his face, and then bought two pints of organic ice cream and several small containers of Greek style yogurt, all of which he devoured in one sitting, in his car in the Whole Foods parking lot. Then he went back to his tower and fell asleep.

God woke up feeling sick and heavy. He decided to skip breakfast and go back to bed, since he still felt overstuffed even 12 hours after his binge. He'd just have to wait it out.

By about 3 in the afternoon, God was feeling ok again. He had drunk plenty of water with lemon and gotten some rest, and was ready to start dealing with reality.

God took a good look at himself in the mirror: the handsome lean frame, those pouty woebegone lips, eyes of love, admirable chest, etc. And He realized: He was God. He didn't have to be lonely any more. So what if it didn't work out with the only man He'd ever loved. He was God, damnit, and He could have anything He wanted. He was the One who had created Adam in the first place, and He decided right then and there to create a new boyfriend for Himself, a perfect boyfriend, someone beautiful, amazing, intelligent, and sensitive, way better than Adam. Why had it taken Him so long to realize this? He'd been so miserable the past few months since the break-up, and His mind had become clouded by all the grief. Now He felt as if He'd just snapped out of a hypnotic trance.

God had created Adam with relatively little imagination, sculpted him out of mud in exactly His own image, made him predictable and pleasing. Now He'd try something new.

Every morning God got up in the dark, rode his bike to the base of a mountain, and hiked up to the top to watch the sunrise. It was exactly like waiting for a lover to show up, a lover who would always arrive, without a doubt. The sun was His favorite thing in the world.

This time, God was determined not to fuck up. Instead of getting His hands all dirty like when He'd created Adam out of mud, God simply snapped his fingers as the first ray of sun shot over the horizon. This ray of light became a being of such great beauty, and so utterly different from God Himself, that He was stunned.

The guy was super hot, really tan, brown nipples, spongy golden hair like sheep's wool cut close to the scalp. He resembled a wild monk who had gone wandering the mountains for a couple weeks without his razor. Lucifer's face was full of smiles, a face loving life, with golden fuzzy stubble. Amber eyes with shards of green, like stained glass windows that had been fucked and shattered by rays of sunlight. God was fascinated and jealous of this face that was so effortlessly happy and free.

Lucifer was the kind of guy who felt at home and relaxed anywhere, and was always bringing joy to everyone. God followed Lucifer around. They would have passionate, unreal sex. God felt worthless compared to Lucifer, and wanted to be Lucifer, so that the relationship quickly became more torturous than being alone.

Lucifer said "I love you" all the time, laughing like an idiot, but he loved everything and everywhere he went he said the same thing to everyone with the same completely vapid laugh. He and God would often go to the beach, chanting and screaming into the ocean until the dolphins came close to the shore and called back.

God called him Satan, the opponent, the enemy.

Reasons why I HATE Satan
a list by God:

1. Satan's beauty is a mockery of everything good in this world.
2. Satan's in love with everyone and I want him to just love me.
3. Everything always works out for Satan.
4. Satan says stupid shit all the time.
5. Satan is fucking HAPPY all the time.
6. Satan thinks he's better than me.
7. Satan is better than me.
8. Satan's hotter than me.

We were driving up a canyon as the sun was starting to set. Lucifer wanted to watch the sunset, and I always do what Lucifer wants.

I pulled over, and we got out and scrambled up the side of the hill. We sat up there, and I started sobbing uncontrollably at the sun's beauty, and Satan's beauty, and the fact that he'll never love me. I thought he had to love me, since I created him out of something I love so much. He says he loves me, but he loves EVERYONE and EVERYTHING so much that it is meaningless. I will never be happy until he needs me desperately, as I need him.

Satan started to laugh hysterically. I wish I could laugh like that, he finds joy in everything. So we sat there on the top of the hill, I'm crying my guts out and he's laughing like an idiot as the sun goes down and people all over the world are murdering each other.

I always thought I was the wealthiest man in the world. I own an enormous tower on a hill, so tall that it penetrates the clouds and exists half in heaven and half on earth. I created everything. I own everything.

Satan owns nothing but he is the wealthiest person alive, because he is at home and in love everywhere he goes. He finds joy everywhere and roams about freely, unattached to anything. I want that.

I decided to take Lucifer to the fanciest rich person's mall in town because I thought he'd get a kick out of it. They have a Christmas tree the size of a skyscraper, full of glass ornaments the size of children, and fake snow blowing around.

I hate being with him. He outshines me wherever we go. And he always strikes up vapid conversation with random passersby and invites them to come along with us wherever we're going. When Lucifer is around, everyone ignores me. I am God, I'm invisible, I don't exist to people. Lucifer is magic, everything he touches is magic, people just instinctively trust him and want to have sex with him. He just has this sexual realness, you know?

Acting normal and having to constantly pull myself together was exhausting me. So I left Lucifer to sit there ridiculously meditating in the food court, and scavenging abandoned pizza crusts on orange plastic trays.

This crazy woman started talking to me at the magazine stand. Probably late 40's but looked younger, suffering and extremely lonely, clearly somewhat delusional. I was feeling so distraught and unworthy and I really wanted to get away from her, but out of kindness I decided to introduce her to Lucifer.

"Let me introduce you to my friend," I told her. "He's a healer."

We went to find Lucifer in the food court. Of course, she was delighted to meet such an attractive and good-natured young guy.

"Wow, you look just like the acupuncturist I used to see when I lived in Italy!" she said to him. She obviously had a huge crush on her acupuncturist. "Your eyes are so clear," she blabbed on, "I can tell you're vegetarian, aren't you?"

Ummmm, excuse me, I'm vegetarian too. I told her so.

"Well, I can tell he's been vegetarian longer, his eyes are so clear," she said.

Actually, I've been vegetarian way longer than Lucifer. I told her so. Gosh, this is getting so petty.

Anyway, the woman said she hated her mother and she suffered so extremely from hating and from the guilt and from all the wounds incurred since birth. Satan told her to forgive her mother and herself, and I told her to let herself hate. She didn't seem to know what to do with all this brilliant advice.

I was ready to leave the mall. Lucifer wanted to start singing so I said fine, ok, because I can't say no to someone so beautiful and he gets really giddy and happy and I just love him so much and wanna make him happy. We started this really terrible, out of tune singing until this security guard told us we had to stop. Lucifer always gets us kicked out of places. Then he convinced me to just meditate with him for 5 minutes under the Christmas tree before leaving the mall.

Just as we were about to sit down under the tree, Lucifer struck up a conversation with a limping elderly man, inviting the man to come meditate with us. It is difficult for me to express how annoying it is when Lucifer extends these kinds of invitations to strangers to enter my personal space. The man started telling us about this leg injury, how he'd been limping around for 6 months, in constant severe pain, etc., etc., yeah growing old sucks, I know, whatever, and next thing I knew, Lucifer told the guy that we'd do a healing. I really wanted to leave the mall urgently, malls drive me crazy unless I'm really in the mood. I can't imagine how I thought it would be a good idea to come here. Any time I take Lucifer anywhere he never wants to leave, he just has so much fun wherever he goes.

Ok fine, so we had the man lie down under the Christmas tree on the fake grass. I stood at the man's feet, Lucifer at his head. I did all the work, while my friend waved his arms around suggestively and smiled like a dumb baby. The old man started to shake and I muttered something about invoking the holy spirit into the body to clear out the demon, etc, count to 10, etc, the man was completely healed and happily ambled away after thanking us profusely.

God's friendship with Lucifer definitely turned out to be even more painful than the breakup with Adam, which God would not have thought possible.

He continued to have fantasies of annihilation, and dreams of being murdered by an intruder wielding an axe. Sometimes it was Lucifer, and sometimes it was a white wolf with bright blue eyes and huge frothy fanged jaws.

One night God awoke from a nightmare in which he had somehow managed to sever all his limbs and head with a kitchen knife, only to find them instantly reappear on his body. Somehow, He could not successfully dismember Himself no matter how hard He tried.

Above all else I am a self, thought God. God rebelled against the thought, but try as He might, there was no escape from what was existing.

I just want peace! God prayed into the empty sky.

What is born of the flesh is flesh. What is born of the spirit is spirit, answered the Void.

"Bullshit!" God screamed.

It was the moment before dawn, and God was covered with sweat. He decided to possess a human being.

The Possession

hile lurking around the empty streets and public spaces of Cologne in the time between night and day, God spotted Sigewize, a female college student, age 20, gazing at a fountain in the town square and admiring the way the starlight reflected off the surface of the water. God violated her and possessed her body.

My name is Sigewize. I am now 20 years old. I live in Cologne with my mother, father, and my little brother and sister, Brandon, age 11 and Elke, age 7. I live in constant fear that my family will die, and I have persuaded my father to lock me in the attic every night to prevent me from murdering them. I am allowed to go outside under supervision, although I don't really notice the difference between being inside and being in nature. I often cannot understand what anyone is saying to me, and I spend my spare time scratching the wooden walls and floorboards of my attic until my fingernails bleed, gagging, laughing and beating my fist against my head when I am not being physically restrained. I cannot feel normal emotions such as sadness, fright, happiness or anger, but I often have a strong intuitive sense that I am experiencing intense panic and dread. I had been attending the University of Cologne up until a few months ago, when my behavior became too disruptive and dangerous to myself and the other students.

At first I became reserved and sullen. Since I was usually bubbling with joy and friendliness, some of my friends inquired about the sudden gloom. My friends were very patient with me at first, but over the next couple weeks all my relationships became tenuous.

I couldn't make sense of anything. When asked about how I felt and what was going on, I had trouble identifying a meaningful answer, and I could only reply with stereotypical sentences such as "I feel alone in this world" and "no one understands, not even I."

I remember sitting in my dorm room one

afternoon with my roommate. She was telling me that she had just uncovered a memory of having been molested as a child. I managed to nod and make sympathetic facial expressions and sounds at the proper times, which was a skill I had developed from watching TV. However, I had no sense of the significance of her words.

I would often wake up in the middle of the night drenched in sweat, blood and fluid the same texture as raw egg, which I understood to be the fluid that is discharged with a stillborn child. One such night I suddenly became conscious that I was making love to my boyfriend, who became terrified at the bloody mess and attempted to interrupt our union. I restrained him in a mighty grip with my legs, and was unable to fight the urge to beat his face with my hands abusively, which drew blood and left scars. In fact, he almost died from choking on his vomit due to my unreasonable jerking pressure on his flanks with my thighs.

Another evening, my friend Daphne was preparing tea for me and some other friends in the common room. She had placed the teacups on a tray and was setting the cups and saucers down in front of us, one by one. As she set my tea down and smiled pleasantly at me, I noticed for the first time that one of Daphne's front teeth was severely chipped, and at the same time I noticed that both my teacup and the saucer each had one very pronounced chip as well. I interpreted this as an unforgivably violent attack on me personally, even though I rationally understood that this was nonsense. I couldn't let go of the feeling that she despised me, saw me as less than a human being, and was determined to accomplish my worst suffering. This was accompanied by terrible feelings of guilt, for Daphne had never treated me with anything other than love and kindness. I consider this incident with the teacup to be the main reason I now hate myself so completely and long so desperately for death.

I ditched class and starved myself all day, while preparing enormous, indulgent feasts to gobble up after dark. I did this for two reasons: first, to console myself for the awful pain I constantly endured, and also to celebrate my "last meal," as I planned to kill myself the following morning. But something always came up to prevent me from following my plan, or I'd forget.

At Daphne's urging, I went to see Dr. Weiß, a psychiatrist at the student health center. I felt immediately relieved as I entered Dr. Weiß's office, with its soft, aqua sofas, bubbling desk fountain and comforting Japanese-style landscape art. I instinctively trusted her and told her everything about all the disturbing changes that had come over me recently, including my attempts to poison Daphne, my preoccupation with suicide, and my lavish nightly "last meals." As I spoke I had the impression that Dr. Weiß didn't understand or believe that I was suffering, since she had a way of chiming in with polite laughter at inappropriate times, such as when I would describe in detail some of my death fantasies. At the end of my session, Dr. Weiß diagnosed me with "mood disorder, not otherwise specified" and prescribed five medications for me in doses which I later discovered were illegal, and often fatal.

After this horrible betrayal by Dr. Weiß, the one person I trusted in the world, I couldn't take any more of this hideous thing that people call "life." I took a dagger and used it to fuck myself between the ribs repeatedly. Then I realized with horror that I was still alive.

I ran into Daphne's room, which she leaves unlocked. Her head symbolizes the impermanence of physical reality, which I removed by force. I carefully left the room.

I, Sigewize, am utterly alone. I am possessed by the

spirit of God, which wants to ruin me. Somewhere inside of me, I am certain that there is a beautiful, lighthearted girl who loves to laugh. I must find this girl, the true Sigewize. I am willing now to wrestle with the spirit of God, for this is the only way that I can find myself.

I entered my boyfriend's loft, where he was still asleep, his breath heaving under that enormous rib cage, so large that I could crawl into it. Everything in that room was askance—twisted sheets, twisted magazines, shirt, sock, empty beer cans, greasy pizza box. I looked at my love, the man's body and the simple sleeping face. I admire that he can sleep late into the afternoon, I myself have not slept for several hundred hours, as I am haunted by the sound of babies shrieking each time I shut my eyes; the sound seems to come from inside my own body. If I could only find that baby, I could feed it what it needs, or murder it and be free.

I tidied up my boyfriend's room. Finally he woke up at around 3pm. I fed him soup, then we took a walk.

The day was beautiful, the grass sparkled like emeralds with clouds floating by like little cotton balls. Only the murkiness of perpetual dissatisfaction and longing for death clouded my heart. My boyfriend was quiet a while. He seemed so lovely, yet so far away, like an enormous dark tower in an inaccessible, nocturnal landscape torn apart by storms and riddled with marshes. Then he explained to me that although he loved me, he'd been unhappy in our relationship for quite some time. He was concerned that I was mentally unstable, and that unless I was able to heal from this awful parasitic affliction that inhabited me, our relationship couldn't work.

My boyfriend—I could never remember his name—then handed me 3 envelopes. The first two he handed me in broad daylight, the third secretly.

The first envelope contained a letter from the assistant to the secretary of the chancellor of the University. The seal was emblazoned in gold and silver at the top. This letter officially banished me from attending school, due to my inhuman behavior and violent deeds, which were described as "unacceptable."

The second envelope contained a somewhat sadistic and ridiculous final love letter from my boyfriend, in which he again confirmed his love, also stating that he no longer desired to see me ever again. Then, as if signing an 8th grade yearbook, he wished me the best of luck in my life's journey.

The third envelope he handed to me with shifting eyes, when nobody was watching. The paper was gray and crumbling, and appeared to contain a map of sorts. The map was shaped like a female breast. I stared at the lines and scribbles, trying to make sense of the damned thing. The boyfriend said goodbye and left.

There I was, all alone at the edge of the wood. So I decided to follow the map.

I hobbled along the path, sobbing uncontrollably. I felt very urgent. Following the map was not an easy task, since I couldn't make any connection whatsoever between this map and this wood. I checked my cell phone out of habit, but there were still no messages. I still half-believed that my boyfriend would call and want to get back together again. I fantasized a conversation with him, in which I told him I would think about it.

Once inside the wood, I forgot my past.

Darkness fell and I became a wild creature. I was now a drooling crone creeping over the forest floor. According to the map, which I still clutched in my gnarled hand, I was almost there. Where is "there?" I had no idea, but I believe the parasitic intelligence inside me, which some would call "divine guidance," was leading me to my destination. I could do nothing but trust, since my body seemed to move on its own like a hungry animal, dirty stomach dragging across the soil sniffing out interesting smells, while my mind existed elsewhere. I stuck my face down and sucked up earthworms and tender green leaves as my only grub.

While in that forest, my body had several consecutive love affairs with young men I met there. Perhaps by coincidence, perhaps not, each one claimed to be a friend of the being that inhabited me. These boys were gorgeous simpletons, which are exactly the types of men I like to fuck. For some reason, the men of this forest found me irresistible, despite my now aged, crumpled appearance and the smells coming from my body.

I miss my boyfriend, the one whose name I can't remember.

One morning, my current lover and I woke up under a tree bedecked with dazzling fruits.

Possessing a human being is very uncomfortable, but worth it because being female, the guys I like want to fuck me, thought God, even though I am now a haggard woman and eat worms straight out of the ground.

Now I remember that Lilith planted this tree in her garden, thousands of years ago. She grew special fruits on this tree, which she called "fruit of the knowledge of good and evil." I have no idea why Lilith grew this tree, just as I have no idea why Lilith does anything that she does. By tasting these fruits, a human being would remember Me and become like Me. And therefore suffer all the time.

While Lilith had tended this absurd tree and slithered around everywhere, Adam had completely forgotten about Me. He had basically become a normal straight dude and did nothing but laze around and make dumb, corny jokes that Eve laughed at like an airhead, while gazing at him with infatuation and doing his laundry.

Even though part of me had wanted nothing more than to watch Adam suffer, I guess I still really did love him, because I felt compelled to protect him.

Eve answered the door. "Oh, just a minute, let me get my husband." She was wearing so much makeup she looked like a fucking cupcake.

Neither of them had any idea who I was. I just told them to stay away from that one tree. I drew a map that resembled Eve's tit, to show them which tree I was talking about.

"Eat whatever else you want, it will keep you young and beautiful and happy. But if you eat the fruit of the knowledge of good and evil, you're screwed and you'll get sick and die. Goodbye." I walked away.

In retrospect I can see I totally overestimated Adam and Eve's intelligence. They had no idea what I was talking about. But since I'd originally created Adam to live forever in perfect pristine joy, I thought I'd give them a shot and warn them.

Lilith seduced Eve, who found that she preferred snake sex to human sex. Then Lilith convinced Eve to eat the fruit, which was the most delicious thing Eve had ever tasted. The juice dribbled down her chin, she noticed she had a body, and she went to the cosmetic surgeon right away and had blush and eyeliner tattooed on her face. She also got injections so she couldn't feel her face anymore, or make expressions.

Eve fed Adam the fruit. Now he realized he had a body. They both became depressed and started to breed, mostly producing large centipedes, but occasionally a human being would come out of Eve's cunt.

Adam would now have sex with me whenever

I wanted. But if there's one legitimate thing I've discovered in therapy, it's that I, God, only desire the unattainable. I had no use for Adam anymore.

"Now I remember where I am," said the being who was both Sigewize and God to her lover. His tan, dolphin-like body needed no clothing or shelter, for he had lived in that forest for thousands of years.

When the sun came up, they smelled breakfast and saw a steeple looming. Sigewize told her lover to hide in the bushes and behave himself 'til the coast was clear. He usually did whatever she asked.

That's all she remembered. She collapsed before she ever reached the abbey.

Part V

The Exorcism

got a phone call from Adelbrand. He was feeling needy again. That meant, I was going to have to get out of this hot tub, where I was having the time of my life with Hildegard and some of the other hot and fun young priestesses, with Arcady massaging my head, get on my bicycle, pedal and pedal in this storm praying I wouldn't get struck by lightning, and then walk the bike through that swamp to go get Adelbrand. He had spent the weekend at Lilith's.

"Why don't you just tell Addie to get over himself and come out here?" Hildegard asked.

I told her he never would, *he's having an episode.* I left, annoyed.

During my bicycle ride, I came across an unexpected object in the street. An old woman had collapsed, shaking, and wolves were howling all around her. She was covered in bloody grime and clutched a map-like depiction of a tit to her wrinkly tit. I called Adelbrand and told him to come meet me, and to bring his car. *It's an emergency.*

We shoved the lady into the back seat. Then we went back to Rupertsberg. The old woman didn't stop shrieking the entire time.

At the castle, all was very silent (except for the mad shrieking). The body hopped out of our arms and bounced up the driveway. Adelbrand and I walked the bouncing body into the house, leaving a trail of bloody fluid. The body bounced so high and the tongue thrust in and out so violently we become concerned for the lavish décor. Rightfully so, for lamps and banisters and things were shattered in the body's path. It bounced a bloody message onto the carpet—SCRUMPILGARD SAVE ME FROM THIS UNCLEAN SPIRIT—

Scrumpilgard and some of her friends came in to see what all the commotion was.

"First of all, you dick, my name's not SCRUMPILGARD," said Hildegard. "And second of all—"

Second of all, Hildegard slapped the woman

really hard to calm her down.

Hildegard grabbed my wrist hard, looked into my eyes and said, "Johnny, I'm going to need you to help me with the exorcism."

I was freaked out but said ok.

We entered the heart.

The heart is a lonely road that leads away from the sun. Words cannot describe how awful it feels to walk down this road. In order to be a person, you must not walk down this road. This is where Hildegard and I now existed. Somehow, I trusted her.

The road was made of iron. A man milked a snowwhite goat by the roadside. Since iron is a material which God holds in disfavor, I was surprised when I recognized that the man is an angel. I could see that the goat represented Sigewize's youth and purity, and the angel was milking the goat to death. This road was so banal.

Finally we got somewhere. It was a castle by the sea, with a central tower dominating the whole sky, phallologocentrically. The top of the tower was impossible to see. Hildegard told me I was about to fall in love. Ok.

"Go into that tower and introduce yourself to God. He is the prince who lives there," she said. I was nervous, but I followed her instructions. This was an exorcism, after all, and I know nothing about exorcisms. So I'd better follow orders. Hildie knew what she was doing.

I went into the tower, where it was midnight. Inside the tower loomed a castle with four spiky towers. It was very claustrophobic and weird in there, for I was neither outside nor inside. Reality. A sad-looking guy was standing around aimlessly, swathed from the top of his neck to his ankles in a black flowing thing like some eccentric, foppish nobleman.

We met face to face. It was an awkward moment, for it must have been obvious I didn't belong there. "Um. . . hi," I said with a nervous giggle. He was kind of cute and morose. I guess he was hot, if you're into emo guys. We started walking together and I blabbered on like a fake teenybopper who's trying to appear cool. He didn't say much. I was uncomfortable. I couldn't tell if he liked me. The more I noticed his face, the more I found him cute, and wanted him to like me. I started feeling very dismal and stopped talking.

We were in a ghost carnival. A ghost carnival is a carnival that has been completely abandoned, usually because of an epidemic outbreak or natural disaster in the county. The carnival was totally empty, with some ghost trash and ghost popcorn occasionally skittering by on the dirt.

Is a human being meandering through life any different, really, from a kernel of popcorn haplessly blowing across the street? I asked myself. I couldn't come up with an answer. The popcorn stopped. Then started again. Then stopped. Just like my eagerness to be here. I really don't like carnivals, especially creepy, abandoned ones in the middle of the night, with chilly wind and a Ferris wheel that creaks around and around slowly. And a kind-of-cute guy who doesn't seem to care about me. I had to remind myself—this is an exorcism, not a date.

"Would you like me to take you on the Ferris wheel?" asked God. The way he said it, I got the feeling that he actually took me to this nightmarish place to impress me and show me a good time.

"What I'd really like," I said, "is for you to take me up to that clock tower and shelter me from this bitter wind."

We climbed a ladder with no end in sight. What is this ladder even attached to? Why am I even here? When I don't know what to say, I ask an unanswerable question.

Finally he took me somewhere I could deal with—a candy store. The shack was situated next to the stagnant waters of a broken fountain, which reflected the black metal of the monstrous roller coasters all around. Every once in a while a car came by overhead, and we could almost hear the shrieks of nonexistent persons.

Most of the bins in the candy store were either empty or contained only empty wrappers and crumbs. God said I could have whatever I wanted. His mood seemed to improve as he watched me enjoy the tiny bits of chocolate I was able to suck out of the wrinkles of ancient candy wrappers. He's pretty cute when he smiles. I had no idea how to act.

The more time I spent around this guy, the more I noticed how cute he was. I think I'm actually starting to fall for this guy.

"I don't really know how to do this," I said to his face. Oh my God, that face is just so cute I can't believe it's actually a face.

"Just be yourself," he said simply.

I tried to be myself. What would I do in this

situation? I would probably act like something. What would I act like? Would I act like I know how to act? I'm not really an actor. I'm more of a dreamer. Worrying exhausts me, and I became so tired I could no longer act fake. Plus we were both finally more relaxed and comfortable around each other. God, I'm so relieved I don't have to act fake anymore. I still couldn't tell if he was really into me, though. At least he was being polite.

We spent the rest of the night walking around a dark lake in a forest, and talking about our lives. We talked easily, as if we'd known each other for years.

When God starts talking about something he's excited about, he gets so speedy and adorable. His energy seems to collapse just as easily, and he stares off into a devastating void. I found it all mostly charming, and I liked him even more as the evening progressed. I had to keep reminding myself why I was there, although I had no idea what I was supposed to do. So I just went along with God.

After some hours passed, God sighed and looked up at the sky. "It's getting late," he said poetically. "Listen, Johann, would you like to stay with me at my cabin tonight? Just to save you the trouble of getting yourself home at this hour. I have a spare bedroom, nothing inappropriate, of course."

For the first time, I realized with panic that I had no idea how I would even get out of this place.

"Ok," I said.

God's cabin was very cute and comfortable, not far from the lake. He tucked me in with a red and brown quilt and I fell immediately asleep. Hildegard visited me in my dream.

I had to walk up 1000 stories and 10,000 marble stairs to a garden where Hildegard was sitting by a tree in the grass, waiting for me, as she coddled a white unicorn. The unicorn was very impolitely gobbling up sweets from Hildegard's hand, and she just laughed and pet the little beast.

Hildegard told me that I was doing a wonderful job, that she thought that God liked me very much, and that she was confident that we would successfully liberate the girl Sigewize from her affliction. She said I should just provide God with companionship for the time being. "Just enjoy yourself, Johnny," she said laughing, as the unicorn tickled her neck with its little tongue.

I woke up a moment before God burst into

the room, looking frenzied and manic.

"Will you do me a HUGE favor, Johann?" He asked.

"Um, what?" I asked, still disoriented from sleep and alarmed at his tone.

God started to blurt something out, then stopped himself. He could tell that his panic was starting to make me panic, so he tried to regain his composure.

He sat on my bed and spoke somewhat slowly, but with a slight nervous quiver. "Listen, Johann. I did something very reckless without thinking, and now I need your help. I've really messed up." Then he looked at me for a response.

"Um... what did you do?" I asked him, because that's obviously what I was supposed to say, but honestly I don't know if I really wanted to know, and I was kind of nervous about where this was going.

"A few months ago," God answered, "just to amuse myself one afternoon, I started to dream up what my wedding would be like. You know, Johann, I've always wanted to get married." Here he gazed dreamily into space. "So just for fun, I started to imagine how I would actually plan the event."

"Ok..." I said.

God went on, his voice gaining speed in little jerks. "I took every care to make this the loveliest, most exquisite event imaginable, I ordered all the food and wedding cake, and hired the entertainment and booked the hall and everything! And then, Johann, do you know what I did?"

"What?" I asked him.

"I had the invitations designed and printed by the finest calligrapher in all the kingdom! Striking violet ink on linen board watermarked with scenes of the seaside. . ." He seemed to nearly swoon as he said this. "And do you know what I did next, Johann?"

"Um, what?"

"I actually sent the invitations out to thousands and thousands of guests! And guess what happened after that!" Now he almost seemed disturbingly cheerful.

I just lay there glaring at him and pulling the covers up around my neck. This was all just making me very tired, and I wanted to go back to bed. God didn't wait for me to respond.

"I completely forgot about the whole thing! Then, this morning, as I was preparing some fresh watercress and licorice jam for our breakfast, I glanced at my calendar and saw I had marked this day to be the day for my wedding!"

God buried his face in his hands and shivered uncontrollably. Then he looked straight into my eyes, as if expecting me to comfort him. I had no idea what to say, so I must have just kept glaring. I felt really bad. It's hard when you're over at the house of a new friend you hardly know, and they're freaking out about something. I didn't really want to get too involved, so I just kind of quietly looked off to the side and waited.

Soon enough, God started pacing the room, now making no effort to conceal the lunatic fear in his voice. "When I saw it on the calendar, I couldn't remember if I'd actually gone through with the whole thing, or if I'd just planned it out as an idle pastime. So I telephoned the Burghotel auf Stachelberg to double check, and I've just been on the phone with the concierge and she says there are over 10,000 people there waiting for the ceremony to start!"

I tranced out staring at the calm lake through the window, wishing I could somehow escape.

"Please, Johann! I can't show up alone, and I can't not go! It would be the end of my reputation." He started to weep and dropped to his knees. "Please, marry me in front of all those people!" God doubled over, and grasped my hand, holding it to his face as if he were going to use it to dry his tears.

"Is this going to be, like, a real wedding, or just a sham so you don't look bad?" I asked. I was honestly just curious, but it came out sounding kind of cold-hearted, which was not my intention.

"I don't know!" God wailed as he bowed his head even lower and pressed the palm of my hand against the top of his head.

Obviously, I couldn't say no. I agreed to marry him.

I would let myself be known as Wilhelmus Glücklich, the name of God's imaginary fiancé printed on all those invitations.

The Exorcism, Part 2:
The Wedding

od's relief and gratitude completely transformed him in a matter of seconds. He showered me with kisses, then looked at my tattered outfit and frowned. "This will never do," he scolded affectionately. Of course, since God is six inches taller than me, I couldn't wear any of his clothes.

"I've just the thing!" he exclaimed. "You're exactly the same size and build as the statue of Saint Eucharius in the chapel." With that, we immediately left the little cabin in a horse-drawn carriage.

God kept himself busy in the carriage, compulsively fixing his bow tie and scrutinizing his reflection in a hand mirror. He kept muttering randomly, and glanced up at me every once in a while with a twinkle in his eye, a kiss, and the words, "My lovely Wilhelmus." At some point I started to question my actual identity. By the time we reached the little chapel God had mentioned, I couldn't recall my previous name. I told myself just to forget about it and enjoy my wedding day. The driver stopped the carriage in front of the chapel and waited. I distracted the friar in the vestibule, while God snuck into the nave and carefully snatched Eucharius' vestment.

Since we were in such a rush, I was forced to dress myself inside the carriage. The garment was black and cream-colored, highly stylized with intricate folds and ribbons, and nicely completed with a little crimson Phrygian cap with a silver bell and a tassel on the end. "Just perfect for a young man on his wedding day," observed God with satisfaction after I was all put together.

We approached the Burghotel auf Stachelberg from behind, past the fountains and up the marble steps. The lobby was a chaos of fancy cologne and perfume smells mingling and old people dressed marvelously but looking completely impotent underneath their spectacular clothing. Chatter filled the hall.

We had a hell of a time trying to figure out which grand ballroom in the Stachelberg was the one that had been reserved for the wedding. God kept asking various hotel personnel, but they seemed to need more information. All he could remember was it was supposedly the grandest of all the grand ballrooms, but apparently there are so many grand ballrooms at Stachelberg. There's the Golden Hall, the Heart Shrine Ballroom, the Whirling Stone Chapel, the Tower of Prisms, the Portuguese Cinnamon Velvet Country Café (which is in fact actually a ballroom), the Royal Badger, the Peacock and Viper, the Topaz Mansion, the Banshee's Heart, and the Dungeon of Kept Promises (also in fact, a ballroom, which takes up three stories, and is perhaps the most lavish of them all, according to the guest services agent we spoke to). And these were only the grand ballrooms in Stachelberg's western wing.

You'd think that when God's having a wedding, every person in sight would be on their way there, but as it happened, these masses were moving about aimlessly in all directions like very slow-moving and unpredictable insects, so it was impossible to tell who to follow. There were some children too, in stiff little suits and dresses they must have hated wearing, ribbons in their hair and sleeves buttoned up tight around their wrists, with their parents all in a muddle trying to make their way across the room. Why do I always think I'm better than everyone? I hate it, but I can't help it. Mostly when I'm tired and irritable, such as when surrounded by chaotic masses of humans. God held me close to him with his hand reassuringly on my shoulder. Please, God, get me out of here.

"Oh, Ma'am?" God suddenly caught the agent by the velvet sleeve as she was about to walk away. "I remember now, it was the Vermillion Gallery!"

"Down that hall and up the stairs, past the baths, through the glass tunnel over the rose and lily gardens and straight ahead!" she answered right away.

He tipped her with a handsome roll of bills and she squealed delightedly, as we sped off as directed. The torches burned bright on the satin-upholstered walls, which barfed up gold fleurs de lys, I can't focus when I'm tired and hungry. God noticed my crankiness and gave me a supportive little cuddle, told me not to worry, little Wilhelmus, the ceremony will be brief and the banquet awaits us. I love him. How I wish we could be done with all this pomp and ceremony and get back to our lives in the country! Or were we lords in a castle? I can't remember any of it, but I just want the honeymoon to start, to be driven everywhere in that carriage, curl up in God's arms, maybe drink some tonic water with lemon and not have to deal with all these bratty crowds!

As we finally approached the Vermillion Gallery, some helpful staff began to arise to take care of us. God and I were separated, which was fine, because I was taken to a large comfy dressing room and invited to lie down on a wonderfully soft and deep cream corduroy couch with silver thread embroidery, to receive my foot massage. It turned out we were actually 15 minutes early. The hotel staff was incredible, and came by to offer me water, wine and nuts, and outfitted me with a handsome sheer white cape with a long train, and a modest solid gold seven-pointed crown that fit snugly over my Phrygian cap.

Of all the galleries and fields of roses and lilies and chambers and halls and glass tunnels we had passed through, the Vermillion Gallery was truly the finest, the most impressive I had ever seen. God certainly knew how to plan a wedding. The walls were leafed in a vermillion shade of gold, with long white pillars like swans' necks arching into the distant domed ceiling and tipped in more gold leaf. All around the dome were giant tear-shaped blue and violet and green stained glass windows that appeared tiny from our perspective on the floor. Guests were sitting everywhere on white or gold couches, on tiered levels reaching up the walls, behind cascades of falling orchids everywhere like waterfalls into the deep marble canals lining the processional. I don't really remember the ceremony clearly, just all those blurred multitudes and bright daylight falling on white candles everywhere, and raining violet orchids and harsh applause. There was an orchestra of harps where I emerged, and on the other side of the hall, an orchestra of French horns. I looked around through this chaos trying to figure out where God was; finally when I reached the center, he was just standing there.

Immediately after the ceremony, we adjourned to the banquet hall. Everyone watched me cut the first piece out of the cake, an architectural masterpiece cloaked in gray frosting that resembled freshly poured cement, with tiers upon balustrades upon Corinthian columns of fragrant icing roses spilling everywhere, even into the bounty of space. Around the cake was a moat of crème brûlée as abundant as all the blood that has ever sustained living beings in all worlds. God and I were impeded in every direction by well-wishers, both marvelous and hideous, trying to congratulate us.

There was all this commotion and excited whispering around a little girl holding a large empty gold platter. Word was going 'round that there was going to be a head offering, for it was customary in this country that a guest should offer his or her head for the good fortune of the newlyweds. Not a requirement, but considered highly auspicious if a guest volunteered to do so. When God realized this was going to happen, his smile was so generous and sincere it seemed to occupy the whole land. "I really wasn't expecting this," he said. I looked around to where some people gathered, in a little section of the hall that was separated with gold cords. The little girl with the golden platter was being led to this area. And in the midst of all the people trying to get everything very organized—I saw, to my amazement, Danny Barnaby, standing in their midst, all dressed up in white and baby blue, and talking to no one. God saw that I was distracted. "Have you never seen a head offering, Wilhelmus?" God asked warmly, with his hand below my neck.

"I see someone I know," I told him. "I'm just going to go say hi." God squeezed the back of my neck and kissed the top of my head, then turned to talk to some guests.

I ran up to Danny. "What are you doing here?" I was really excited and shocked to see him here, and also happy to be able to share the joy of my special day with him. He looked happier than I'd ever seen him.

"Johnny, hey! I had no idea you were the one getting married to God until I saw you walk up the aisle!"

"It's Wilhelmus now," I corrected him. We just couldn't stop smiling at each other. "But how did you get here?" I asked.

Danny started talking really fast, like there was so much that had happened since I saw him last that he'd never have time to explain everything. He told me about how he had stayed in the City of the Pyramids for an immeasurable amount of time, cleaning and serving each day for all the beings there. He hadn't been expecting to ever leave, but one day the prince of the city came and gave him a key to God's realm, as an honorarium for all his faithful service. Danny had also received a wedding invitation.

"But I always thought you hated God," I said, confused.

"Johnny, I realized that God is suffering as much or more than all of his pathetic creation. I wanted to give him something. I'm so happy for you, Johnny. I'm offering my head for your total success and happiness together. I know how long you've wanted this."

"What, it's YOU? The head offering?" I was horrified and confused, but Danny was just beaming generously at me. I tried to smile gratefully for a second, but it was such a painful effort.

Just then there was a commotion behind Danny, and some people trying to get his attention. It looked like it was time for the offering. There was a man with a jeweled sword and some attendants, and the girl with the golden platter, waiting. Waiting. Just like we're all waiting for death.

Danny looked elated. At the same time, there were speeches and toasts going on, one after another aging persons making jokes that weren't funny or else I didn't understand them, but the whole crowd would laugh jovially, as if they were all the best of chums. Finally, after a number of these speeches, the swordsman cut off Danny's head. But because of all the formalities going on, they weren't ready to actually make the offering yet. So Danny had to just stand there with his severed head balancing on his neck. He was getting noticeably uncomfortable. Actually, Danny was starting to look like his old self again, holding his abdomen and squirming, as he impatiently asked the nearby attendants if he could make the offering yet. I saw what was going on, and told him I'd see what I could do. Two women were standing there and pointing at his face, which was getting dark and wet with spots, like an old banana. "We should really get someone to take the fat out of that," one of them said. Danny's situation was looking more and more grim, and whereas a moment ago he'd seemed so happy and relaxed, now he was looking more and more paranoid and uncomfortable. The decomposition didn't help things.

The toasts and formalities were still going on. It was so boring, like being at a graduation ceremony or something. Old people getting drunk everywhere. I hated that, as a groom, I had to smile politely at people. I could not force myself to laugh at their embarrassingly dumb jokes, however. That would have been just too much.

I went to God to see if he could intervene with the proceedings, cause I was worried about Danny. But it was kind of typical, Danny was always getting himself into some kind of trouble or another, usually self-generated. I still felt bad for him, having to stand there waiting through all that endless jabber, trying to keep his body from falling apart. But this poor human body, made of the simple elements, falls apart eventually. Inevitably.

God spoke to a couple of important-looking people, then came back to my side. I caught him by the collar and kissed him on the cheek. "Can we go?" I whispered in his ear. I wanted to get the hell out of there and carry on with our married life together.

Just before we slipped out of the hall through a secret back curtain, I saw that they were carrying out the head offering. For a moment I wanted to run back for Danny—I thought maybe God and I could adopt him, or Danny could live with us and be in charge of making our breakfast every day, or something—anything—but it was too late, and God pulled me close and whisked me out the door.

As we ran down the Burghotel's marble steps, bells chimed from every sunlit tower in the land, for the Lord had just been wed. We fled by limousine with dark windows. I hardly noticed the gorgeous, lush scenery of the countryside streaking by, as God kept me entertained by feeding me rich foods and lovingly stroking my body. He thanked me over and over again as we made out, and then I had dreams of bliss and luxury in His arms. As I revived, we were pulling up to a chateau after dark.

Hildegard and Adelbrand came out to meet us. They were whispering swiftly. Adelbrand babbled like a child, asking so many questions I could scarcely answer one before he asked five more. I made them call me Wilhemus Glücklich.

Sigewize defecated on the floor and passed out. Then she was fine. She ordained as a nun, and ran away to live the rest of her days in prayer in the forest.

A Weird Summer

he exorcism took its toll on Hildegard, who became sick and had to remain in bed a lot. She also got crabby, and started to make absurd decrees that really darkened the mood around the castle. For example, all windows were to be covered by several layers of red cellophane and never opened. All leftover food should remain on the table to rot in its natural state, for to reject the natural state of things was an offense to God. At a certain point, Hildegard demanded that some of the guys lift her out of bed and stuff her under it with blankets and stuffed animals. She remained there for several weeks eating only hand-polished black sesame seeds. She babbled something about a zealous red head appearing in the corner of the room, where the two walls come together, telling

her to do this. Oh Hildegard, you're SO weird.

Of course, after a couple weeks living in those rooms filled with somber red light and moldy food with baby flies and maggots, etc, people started getting uneasy. Some of us got rashes, or boils, or wasting diseases, or just plain hysterical. I myself fell into a deep depression. I even found myself missing God, who had dissolved blissfully into space without saying goodbye, after the exorcism. Nothing felt right at all anymore.

At that time, Josh and Arcady departed for a voyage to South America. They never said so directly, but their departure obviously had to do with the grim changes at the castle. I accompanied them to the harbor and wept and waved goodbye as the ship went out to sea. I felt more abandoned than ever, like I'd lost everything.

Hildegard would spend most of the day in prayer and silence and was obsessed with fasting. She attended Mass eight times a day beginning at two in the morning. She became boring to be around, at best, and we grew apart during that time. Then suddenly one day, Hildegard announced that she had founded a new monastery in dreams, about a half mile away from our mansion, on the site of some dilapidated ruins we had discovered ages ago. She said she was moving there, and left that very hour, taking nothing but a few docile girls who begged to be her attendants.

I was sad to see her go, but also relieved. Mostly, I just hung out with Adelbrand. We were always walking up and down Main Street, imagining that we were having adventures or spying on the regulars in the coffee shop, but they were so unintriguing. It was really a quiet, depressing summer.

Does this mean that if I want a boyfriend, I have to settle for someone like him? Sometimes in the murky light at supper time, or from a very specific 3/4 angle, or when he's in a certain mood and his face shines, then he looks almost cute. Almost. Then if I get closer, I know I don't want to kiss him. I think ever.

Here's what's cute about Adelbrand. And what's not cute. His eyebrows and eyes are actually very cute. His mouth is actually adorable. His arm bones are cute. His phone voice is kind of cute, the way the ends of words sound like he's run out of his voice. Sometimes he comes up with a cute idea, like when he told me he wanted to go swinging from the bell in the bell tower and then he did it. That was cute that he actually did it.

Here's what's not cute about Adelbrand. His skin tone is not that cute. He has too many zits. One zit once a month on a guy with generally gorgeous skin can be cute. Adelbrand simply has too many zits. His negativity is not cute. His hair is wispy and awkward. Not cute. His sporadic facial hair and whining are not cute.

"Why do you want to kiss me so badly?" I asked him one night when he was drinking some red wine and being very persistent and obnoxious to make up for his lack of confidence.

"Because your lips are beautiful," he replied, "and so are mine."

That was totally cute. I tried to kiss him, but I just couldn't really do it. I just don't know how to kiss if I'm not feeling it.

One night we went walking across the bridge that goes over the Rhine, from downtown to the wealthy suburbs. About halfway down the bridge, he put his arm around me. I didn't know what else to do so I let him. It was ok, but it didn't really feel like anything. I don't think it was fair that I let him. It made me hungry for an avocado.

Adelbrand. Adelbrand. Adelbrand. I'm so not obsessed with you. Why can't someone I'm obsessed with be obsessed with me?

I feel bad saying it, but I only spent so much

time with Adelbrand because there was nothing else to do. Like when some other kids went hiking. We both hate hiking, so we sat around eating toast and watching dumb videos on Youtube. Then later we took a bunch of holy basil and ended up sleeping cuddled in a heap. For all I complain about Adelbrand, he never puts pressure on me to act a certain way or be in a certain mood. I know I'm breaking his heart, and I do feel awful about it.

Josh and Arcady sent me postcards every day, one in the morning and one in the afternoon. The postcard in the morning was hand delivered by Renaud, a dapper courier we knew from town. The evening postcard was delivered by a white eagle whose wingspan easily exceeds my height, and whose frightsome beak clapped together and then loudly tapped the window to let me know that he's arrived. I would proudly thank the fearsome white eagle, then throw myself onto one of the divans in the parlour to read the card with glee. This evening, the postcard had a photo of two lemurs holding hands and sitting on chaise lounges in the sun, wearing sunglasses and sipping lemonade through straws. The postcard read:

Dear Johann,

Missing you much. Maybe next time you'll accompany us, for our conversation gets commonplace very quickly without your fresh wit and commentary.

Love You Always,

Josh & Arcady

They each signed and drew little mad smiling faces.

I tried to prevent Adelbrand from seeing me get these little love notes, but it's very difficult to conceal. He's so mopey sometimes and he sort of half-tries to hide it, but it's obvious. At first he would just casually say, "Oh, who's that from?" and then act all unaffected when I told him. But I could tell it upset him. Oh Adelbrand, if only you were hotter and held it together.

I visited Hildegard once, but it was pointless because we never had anything to say to each other anymore. I missed her, the way things used to be.

One night in the heart of that summer, at an obscure hour, when a circular wind was swirling around the house, and the only sounds I could hear in my parlour were the chaotic rappings of branches, leaves and clumps of dirt on the windowpanes, I got up and walked downstairs. All I was wearing were some boxers, cause it was so hot. No one was around. I started eating some crackers in the kitchen, where the moon gleamed like a ghost. I was spacing out, then suddenly saw a tall, fair-skinned, male being appear behind the glass door leading out to the terrace. His crimson regalia shone like dry blood and the glass shattered. He presented me with a bloody thigh bone which produced a puddle of blood on the floor just inside the door. Then he bowed with great pageantry and told me unemotionally that my best friend Hildegard was extremely ill, and that if I ever wanted to see her alive again I should probably hurry over to her monastery without much further ado. I glared viciously at this obscene gentleman, who was most likely a demonic or angelic lover that Hildegard had sent to deliver her message. I knew her type: cute but spidery, with a great nobility of stature. Yes, it was Hildegard's thigh bone. Yes, her body had been ravaged by illness and her mind torn apart by insanity. I learned this all from the apparition.

My body pumped full of adrenaline, I threw some essentials into a satchel and hit the road. By the time I got back downstairs, there was no sign of the guy—only the puddle of blood, broken glass, and gaping open doorway letting in the evil wind. I scribbled a quick note letting everyone else know where I'd gone and why the door was blown apart, and taped it onto the kitchen counter so it wouldn't blow away.

As I stepped outside, I had to fight the wind that was making my progress across the yard very difficult, plastering tiny bits of bark and so forth onto my face.

When I reached the monastery, the place was all dark, except for a little lamplight in Hildegard's window. Was she really going to die?

I ran into the door and into Hildegard's room. She was asleep, and the patches of skin under her eyes were black and spongy. The blankets over her right thigh were stained with dark blood. There was a girl sitting in a creaking rocking chair in the far corner in the dark, doing rosaries. She ignored me when I came in, so I went over to her and asked her about Hildegard's condition. She was chanting rhythmically, maniacally. She never looked up at me, but answered in the same overwrought, restrained voice as her chanting, only a little louder: "Hildegard is very ill, we believe she is dying," and then returned to her prayer. I went to Hildegard's side.

My friend opened both eyes wide, looked straight at me, and said loudly, "Go get the red medicine from Saint Dymphna's tomb. Come back in three days, no later. And I'll be fine."

I just stood there dumbfounded for a few seconds, as I usually do when someone gives me direct instructions which completely overwhelm me. Her red mouth creaked opened and said even louder, "GO NOW!" Then, suddenly, she sighed and fell back asleep.

I went home, beyond exhausted. I would have to get some rest before I could accomplish anything, but sleep was miserable. What was I going to do? Finally, after a couple hours, I passed out.

Page Coin came to me in my dream, walking out of a mist on a lonely road. He was wearing his green-black traveling cloak fastened at the throat with a chaotic basilisk fibula, blackish gnarly boots, a patch with a weird anarchist or magickal sign/logo on it, short hair pointing out every way from under the hood. He looked way more serious than before. Like he'd been through a trauma and was hotter. When we'd met, all those distant years or months or lifetimes ago at Whole Foods, his conversation had made him boring and hideous to me. Now, for some reason, something hidden about him was developed and I could almost kiss him.

"I'm sorry I didn't come sooner," he said. "I gave away all my belongings. I have nothing any longer. I wanted to find you, Johnny. Since I last saw you, I've crossed worlds."

"I need your help, Page," I told him. He agreed to help me, since he had given up all ambition. *This guy is a true knight*, I thought to myself.

During this dream encounter, I told him where he could find me on earth. I told him how to get to our château, and to come right away.

Page Coin arrived at the château later the next afternoon. I was sitting on the veranda outside my bedroom, feeling totally overwhelmed and paralyzed about getting my shit together for this task. I could see down the road, mostly mist and branches obstructing. Suddenly, there he was, just like in the dream.

I felt reassured by Page's calm sense of purpose, which, he explained, was merely the side effect of renunciation of all hope and fear. He believed what people were saying about apocalypse, that any moment the world could cave in under a mass of fire, or the earth beneath our feet would crack and break away and tear off leaving us with nothing to cling to but our own greed. Page Coin was over it. Fearless and/or suicidal.

The Quest

ourneys terrify me. I never know who I am or what I need from one moment to the next. If I can get somewhere, I think I'll be okay. Going is treacherous.

I am afraid of sunset, for the beetle of night is greater than the lion of day. What will I do when the sun falls?

Adelbrand forged the way ahead of us, hacking through the branches and tree trunks that barred our way, with his trusty sword.

Adelbrand, where are you going? You don't know what you're doing. Let Page tell us where to go. He's been across the worlds. I started to run to catch up with Adelbrand, but Page held me back.

"Wait, don't distract him. He's going to lead us, we need him. A mortal of pure mind and heart, only he can get us there." If Page wasn't holding my arm, I swear I'd have run up to Adelbrand and swiped that sword from him.

"Fine," I sulked. I swear Adelbrand is totally clueless. But I trust Page. I guess I'm just going to have to trust.

Adelbrand hacked through thick branches and serpents as thick as children's torsos, just as God cut the original serpent in two through his contempt. These two serpents give us power to travel, Page explains. At this time we are completely encumbered by masses of branches and the split serpents writhing around that Adelbrand has left behind him as waste. Waste is knowledge, Page explains. The deeper we climb through this wood, the closer bugs and branches scrape.

Is it day or night? Above us no sky is apparent, just branches crossing and leaves and slithering snake bodies and birds and squirrels darting through. Adelbrand apparently has lost all fear and knows what he's doing.

Young adventurers, whether timid or bold, can easily lay waste the high mountains, tear up the forests, hack apart the wild animals, and erode all the richness from the soil of the valley. In this way we left a trail of poverty and death where'er we went.

"Don't worry Johnny," said Page. "The only way actually to be born is through annihilation." His words only made me hungry.

We found a little tavern in a thicket where they served mostly beer and pizza made with pig cheese. I thought of Josh's disapproval whenever I ate dairy. I decided not to eat the pizza so I sat there watching Adelbrand and Page scarf down their nasty grub and burp while I sipped on ice water with contempt.

Next morning, Adelbrand sprang right out of bed, leaving me really cold on one side. I clung more tightly to Page, wrapping my legs around him. Adelbrand immediately returned to his hacking and destroying this growth, so that we could continue on our way to save our dying friend.

Adelbrand was wearing a long pin-striped cape that was dirty and tattered. He had dirt on his face and looked sexy. Page Coin had his green velvet cloak, silver fibula pins fastening it together, a shirt with chains on it, and short hair. I was wearing a ruffled billowy shirt but at the last minute I looked in the mirror and felt tired of it. I changed into a wife-beater, some black jeans and boots. On our bodies and clothes we all had dirt streaked, which mingled when we slept in a huddle each night. We could only sleep for about fifteen minutes each time, because we were in such a rush. That morning I woke up with Page and Adelbrand's sweat and saliva on me. Pretty soon to look at Adelbrand's face you were looking mostly at dirt. Same with Page. Adelbrand's cape was practically black now, and translucent from being soaked with dewdrops and sweat. He had rips in his shirt. Page Coin's short blonde hair, like grass, was sticking everywhere.

The next day Adelbrand was wearing some leaves and some spiders were hanging out in the ripped holes in his cape. Page was wearing large thorns in his cloak, and I had vines wrapped around my legs and torso, trying to strangle me. After many days and hours, not a single one of us was wearing a shirt. Blood and dry bruises everywhere, we had parts of our skin that were thinner showing blood and organs and everything. Then we went for so long we almost didn't remember where we were going, but we kept moving in that direction which Adelbrand revealed. I was so caught up in the forest green and my traveling buddies and my own body moving almost without a will, and the glistening parts of wet leaves that were like stars everywhere, that I didn't totally recall what we were doing. But Adelbrand blazed on ahead. Now his cape contained a large shredded hole through which his tan back coated with dirt and grime shone, with shoulder blades dramatically poking out and spreading like wings of bats. I continued to follow his back, which I found that I desired. Page Coin stomped by my side and sang in a voice that made the branches crack and burn. The back of Page's neck, all sinewy and cool, was what I also desired. Myself, I found that my entire bare chest, no longer any difference between my sweat and the gleaming moisture on the vines, wasn't cold any more, including my nipples which had somehow grown larger and more striking. Adelbrand prodded us with his sword tip. My desire increased, and I moved faster.

Finally, the soles in our boots couldn't really be called soles, for the thorns and wild animals had ripped them to shreds. Our feet were covered with so much dirt it seemed as if we were submerged in a tomb. We could possibly no longer be said to be wearing pants or clothes either. Adelbrand had on only sparse pinstripe threads sticking to his back and arms and buttocks like a scribble. His entire back side gleamed with majesty in the light of fireflies. Page's short hair was all tangled up and black, with cobwebs. His eyes had a bright blue sheen. Leaves were plastered on his throat and the backs of his thighs. Our movement had a rhythm that bones were communicating and had their own soul. I know they felt it too, the desire and ease of movement. They kept looking at me, Adelbrand would strike the tip of his sword into my tough intercostal spaces and laugh, his face was now entirely with a dark brown sheen with bright hazel and gold eyes. I clutched his scapulae many times, but we never lost any speed. We had stopped sleeping days ago.

At last, Adelbrand was wearing a hauberk of silver-tipped thorns, Page Coin had his hauberk of live scorpions, and I also emerged from that wood clad in a hauberk of scissor blades that resembled flowers.

We set out over the hill, I in front, Page behind me, and watchful Adelbrand darting back and forth like a fierce Jack Russell. The pine needles cracked in the chill and the sun lingered just below the horizon. We had been journeying all through the day and night because time was precious and Hildegard's life was dangling from a string. At some point in the delirium of hunting continuously, sleeplessly, becoming strong from the little mushrooms we gathered in the forest, the sunlight began to pour through the trees.

The hill had come to meet us across the plains. These wild regions were beyond reason, for the hill was creeping on many legs or pillars, over the sea.

"We must avoid the evil reptiles that hunt these waters," said Adelbrand in the language of the forest. During this journey, he had grown up to become a charming man and shone like a bronze heirloom.

"I have no fear for reptiles, for in this reliquary that I call a heart dwell monsters far more loathsome than those," I replied in a language resembling the snarls and moans of a lucky/poisonous eel.

Page Coin spread his magic cloak over the waters and we safely passed beneath the hill. The ceiling was crawling with moths and rotting things. Adelbrand helped Page and me to mount the underside of the hill.

Mounting a moving hill is nauseating.

The dry wind bit at our bloodshot faces, and we approached the hill's barren crest, which was practically covered by a huge monster who was spazzing so violently he looked like a blur. Among his appendages, I could get a glance at

Saint Dymphna's tomb. The emblem was of a princess holding a sword high in her right hand, while her left hand held the devil on a leash. From the devil's eyes sprang golden rays that created worlds. But I didn't have a chance just then to take in the magnificent details of the stonework, for that monster was trying to kill us. Every once in a while, the rascal stopped flailing and froze for two seconds, so we were able to get a look at him. His arms were dragons, and his legs were giant squids. His belly was an expanse of dry soil at midnight, on which children were screaming and murdering each other. He had 10 eyes which scrambled chaotically across his face like irritated cockroaches. Many times each second, his long, club-like tongue would dart out. On the tongue was heaped a poisonous mound. From his hound-like ears, heartbroken maiden infant-killers' wretched screams and loud sighing rang out, causing much disorientation among anyone who could hear them. Each hair on the monster's body was a long whip, which, as if made of steel, lashed out incorrigibly. From bleeding slits in the monster's scrotum tumbled delicately-limbed venomous spiders wielding long knives. They pranced around and struck poses among the grass, to create a diversion. This wasn't going to be easy. The three of us stood there staring at the monster for a few seconds, with crackles falling perilously close to our eyeballs.

"There is no way to kill this beast," I declared. We darted into the forest not knowing what to do. Maybe we'd have to sacrifice our lives to claim the medicine. We would do that for our friend. However, could there be another way?

We were coughing up dust and prickles of blood, but we made it to the nearby town of Gheel, in the shadow of that hill. In the distant part of the town sat a hermitage among the skeletal building foundations. We consulted the town crone.

"That creature was created from the cause of a man who killed a princess, therefore you must find a lock of hair of a princess who is about to be claimed by death," said the crone.

We were to steal a lock of the princess' hair and have it baked into a scone in the local bakery. With this as our weapon we could somehow defeat the monster, in a way which would be revealed. At least, that's what the crone suggested, and it was our only hope.

The only way to gain access to such a princess was to proclaim ourselves traveling medicine men. It wasn't really a lie, we reasoned, for we were traveling in search of medicine.

Princess Fleur was a shrewd and hilarious cackling sort, who made merry and was always joking, despite her grave illness that caused her skull to make a frightful impression in the flesh of her face. I took off my shoes and slipped into her bed with her for our consultation. I explained everything to her. She gave her hair willingly, and we promised to bring her the red medicine we would soon recover from St. Dymphna's tomb.

We brought the lock of white hair to the baker, a Frau Köhner. We slipped the hair into her scone, unknown.

We had no money, for we creatures of the wild generally have no use for nor understanding of symbolic wealth, our wealth is the gold of the sun, the silver of the dried morning twigs, the fine silk of the winds, and the blood of our enemies, which we drink as wine. Frau Köhner was only too happy to give us the scone in homage to our charm and passion, for our eyes had become irresistible.

We returned to St. Dymphna's hill. Immediately, Adelbrand ran up to the monster and threw the hair cake before it, where it sparkled in the sunlight.

The monster's head sank to the ground to

gobble up the scone and just then, we would have to cut it with a large blade. But no large blade was there to cut. I ran around him with a scalpel. Brother made his way around with a shovel.

Finally, a small figurine appeared on top of the hill. A running shape, it was Danny Barnaby, running in madness. He was now omnipresent and could produce himself wherever he cared in order to be of help. In his right hand he held a sword and in his left his own head, turned upside-down. From the neck gushed many fountains of blood. Following closely behind him was a flock of birds drinking the blood droplets as they were able. So endless were these fountains, they seemed to never run out, and his body and head lacked no luster. In fact, he looked better than ever. His body had really acquired a great ease of form, and his face was handsome and full of bliss. Yet something of my old friend remained, the uncompromising effort as he now ran over the hill. Just before Danny got to the monster, he set his head down on the ground and prostrated to it three times. Then he picked it up and threw it into the monster's neck. After that, he took his sword and speared the monster's intestines, lifting the sword with the stomach dripping down. Of course, the monster was still not even half dead, and its limbs and pores of its skin danced and cackled with murderous delight. Danny then threw his own body onto the monster, which then copulated with him and that was all that there was for many days and nights until one day, a prim small girl in pink with a parasol and nutmeg on her apron arose from the valley and in the silence that accompanied her, passed out vials of medicine to each of us. Then she handed Adelbrand a special one full of the red medicine of the moon, that Hildegard needed to heal. Adelbrand put the medicine into his satchel. Slowly we turned our back on the scene, as the sun had already set and was about to rise again, but perhaps not for many hours. Adelbrand and I sobbed and shivered on the bloody ground, such was the madness of trauma to our poor brains. The little girl with the parasol accompanied us as far as the lily-white lake. She tapped the tip of her parasol onto a stone and a boat appeared with a boatman who did as she wished. We boarded the boat and the little girl disappeared beneath the waves. On the boat we all got reacquainted with each other. I discovered many things about Adelbrand that had been unknown. He had actually been a celebrated sculptor at the court of Athens. Everyone looked more real now. Danny's body had no resistance to anything or anyone. I longed to hold and wrap my arms around it. That. Next thing we knew, we had reached the shore, definitely.

Dragon Earrings &
Nightshade Liqueur

ur little party reached Hildegard just at the turn of the devil's hour, about half past 3pm. Marabel, Hildegard's attendant, received us at the door and took us to her. She was lying out on the chaise lounge by the pool. Her skin was dry like a stone in the sun. Her color was poor, but she looked happy to be sunbathing.

Adelbrand held out the vial to her. "Whatever is in this vial, I assure you, is worth all our efforts and our wishes for you to be well, m'lady." he said and bowed. Adelbrand could be seriously socially awkward, even more so than me at my worst. I held up Hildegard's head, for she had almost entirely lost her body's strength. Each time her body part was moved, a thin layer of dust took flight from its skin and floated away. That was how sick she looked. With my other hand I opened her mouth, which was vaguely smiling, although her eyes were half elsewhere. She looked directly into my skull, with doubtful recognition.

Adelbrand turned the vial upside down and tapped it so the little drops of red liquid reached her throat. Page and Danny stood around with hands on our shoulders, to show their support. Princess Fleur, who had completely recovered during the journey (due to the medicine), frolicked with the ducks in a nearby pond.

Hildegard closed her eyes and lifted her finger, a sign that Marabel was to take her to bed. Marabel then rang her bell, and more attendants came out and carried Hildegard away. A half hour nap later, and my friend was back to her old self. She looked like a desirable human again and could make normal eye contact, and converse as usual.

I grabbed Hildegard's old emerald crown from the bedside table and swiftly placed it on her head. Then I held her hair and hands, with love streaming through our fingers.

What did we talk about? We talked about the cucumbers growing in the garden, about the moss on the trees, about worlds. Mostly, we talked about old times. About times to come. About non times. About no places. About Place to Exist, which was a new restaurant in town. We talked about dragon earrings and nightshade liqueur and griffins that tear up the countryside with their claws. We spoke intimately about many things. Things I don't feel like recounting. We spoke until the day was night and then again, until the sun came up. Then we took a long nap, over 13 hours in length, in Hildegard's bed, all five of us.

When I finally woke up, it was only in Danny's arms. His head was completely intact, his eyes were full of luster, and his breath was like a phenomenal rose that gives birth to a diamond. And I was lucky enough to find that rose. Danny's body was completely new. Each moment it was regenerating. Each evening it turned to a brazen steed, and in the morning again into a divine lover. We would often wake up as each other, or sometimes as one body without front, back, or dimensions.

All things possible and impossible were happening at once, and we were able to share our sublime fortune with all our companions, all the creatures of the forest, and even with all our enemies. And that is how Adelbrand, Page, Josh, Arcady, my dear Hildegard and I lived out the rest of our days.

Notes

Notes

Notes